The Mane Event

Adapted by Perdita Finn

Based on the screenplay by Meghan McCarthy

Little, Brown and Company
New York ✶ Boston

Little, Brown and Company

Hachette Book Group
1290 Avenue of the Americas, New York, NY 10104
Visit us at lb-kids.com

Little, Brown and Company is a division of Hachette Book Group, Inc.
The Little, Brown name and logo are trademarks of Hachette Book Group, Inc.

The publisher is not responsible for websites (or their content)
that are not owned by the publisher.

First Edition: October 2014

Library of Congress Control Number: 2014945044

ISBN 978-0-316-24777-1

10 9 8 7 6 5 4 3 2 1

RRD-C

Printed in the United States of America

For friends who overlook each other's mistakes, differences...and those times when they accidentally turn into world-conquering devil-monsters

CONTENTS

✷ ✷ ✷

CHAPTER

1

All the Wrong Notes

✦✦✦

Teenagers streamed in and out of the fast-food hangout next to Canterlot High School, happily chatting with their friends. They were talking about soccer practice and dance committees and gossiping about the newest couples. They were also buzzing about the Sonic Rainbooms' new song.

"A friend for life is what we want to be!" sang a cheerful group of girls strolling out of the restaurant. With French fries and drinks in hand, the kids hurried off to do homework, waving good-byes and texting last-minute messages. No one noticed the three bickering new girls who left the restaurant without buying a single thing to eat.

Adagio Dazzle, irritated, tossed her lush mane of pastel-colored hair. Aria Blaze let out a dissatisfied sigh that sounded just like a whinny, and Sonata Dusk stomped her foot, discovering that human shoes did not make the same satisfying *clomp* as pony hooves.

A wisp of fluorescent green light wove in between the girls as they slumped against one another. As it wound around their heads, each girl slightly opened her mouth and seemed to drink in a tiny sip of the strange light. For a moment, the scarlet pendant hanging around each girl's neck seemed to glow.

"That was barely worth the effort," complained Aria. "I'm tired of fast food. I need a meal."

"What did you expect?" said Adagio. "The energy in this world isn't the same as in Equestria. We can only gain so much power here."

Aria pouted and sighed again. "I wish we'd never been banished to this awful place!"

"Really?" said Adagio, her voice dripping with sarcasm. "I love it here."

"For realsies?" snipped Sonata. "Because I think this place is the worst."

"I think you're the worst, Sonata," Aria shot back at her.

Sonata's face turned red with fury. "Oh yeah? Well, I think you're worser than the worst, Aria."

"Yeah?" Aria turned her back on the other girls and stared out at the street. "I'm kinda busy right now. Can I totally ignore you some other time?"

Adagio practically snorted with rage. "I'll tell you one thing: Being stuck here with you two isn't making this world any more bearable."

Suddenly, underneath the normal evening noises of teenagers, cars, and music, each girl began to hear a strangely familiar hum. It was pleasingly pitched and just barely audible, so faint that no one else even realized it was there. But the girls heard it, and all three of them instantly turned toward the horizon.

That's when they saw it. In the distance, just beyond the fields of Canterlot High, was the faintest ripple of magical, rainbow light.

Adagio's eyes widened greedily. Beside her,

Aria and Sonata were so thrilled they could barely breathe. The three girls were transfixed by the beautiful colors illuminating the sky.

Adagio was the first to speak. "Did you feel that?" she asked the other girls in a hushed voice. "Do you know what that is?"

The other girls couldn't bring themselves to admit it. How could it be? It wasn't possible.

But Adagio couldn't contain her excitement. "It's...it's...Equestrian magic!"

Aria shook her head in disbelief. "But this world doesn't have Equestrian magic."

"It does now!" Adagio knew what she'd seen. For whatever reason, however it had happened, this ordinary, human realm had Equestrian magic, and she was already hatching a plan. "And we're going to use it to make everyone in this pathetic little world adore us!"

CHAPTER

2

Pitch-Perfect Ponies

✶ ✶ ✶

A few months earlier, Twilight Sparkle had traveled through a secret portal. She was the first Equestrian pony to come to Canterlot High. Sunset Shimmer had stolen her tiara and whisked it away to the human realm in the hopes that she might use its magic to become all-powerful. But Twilight showed her that being a princess is not about having everyone else bow down to you, it is about inspiring those around you to stand at your side.

And that's what happened when Twilight's human friends fought alongside her, using the Elements of Harmony. Applejack's honesty, Fluttershy's kindness, Pinkie Pie's laughter, Rarity's generosity, and Rainbow Dash's loyalty created a powerful rainbow of joy that swept the crown, which was warped with disharmony, from Sunset Shimmer's head and returned it to Twilight Sparkle.

By working together, something enchanting happened to the six friends—they ponied up! First, pony ears appeared, then their hair became full and lustrous like manes, and finally, their tails started swinging! They could be part pony and part girl at the same time!

Sadly, the human girls had to say goodbye to Twilight Sparkle. The beloved pony princess needed to return to Equestria, and the portal between the worlds was destroyed forever. Even after Twilight left, the sparkling rainbow light continued to swirl through the halls of Canterlot High. It seemed to help everyone get along, and it even inspired the girls to start their own band and create music.

Music seemed to pour out of the Equestria Girls after their adventures with Twilight Sparkle. They wrote songs as they whizzed around town in Rarity's convertible and giggled together at the Sweet Shoppe. Rainbow Dash loved to play her guitar almost as much as she loved playing sports. Applejack was a marvel on the bass, and Rarity tickled every key of her keytar. Fluttershy had discovered that she was a natural with a tambourine, and Pinkie Pie poured all her energy and enthusiasm into wild drum solos. The Sonic Rainbooms rocked, and best of all, when the music took over, the girls would pony up!

Hey, hey, everybody,
We're here to shout
That the Magic of Friendship
Is what it's all about!

Everyone at Canterlot High did the Pony Stomp when the Rainbooms played. They crossed their arms and swayed from side to side. They lifted their knees and pranced.

They jumped and clapped. No one could resist them! Not even the Great and Powerful Trixie. Not even Sunset Shimmer!

The Sonic Rainbooms' music was magic, and every time they performed, more of their rainbow energy seemed to shine through Canterlot High. Only one thing was missing—and that was Twilight Sparkle. What would it be like if she were singing with the Rainbooms? They couldn't help but wonder, even though they knew it would never happen. Still, they were happy and everyone at Canterlot High was happy, too, happier than they'd ever been. But little did they know that a force of discord had just arrived in their world....

CHAPTER

3

Sunset Shimmer's Blues

✶ ✶ ✶

Canterlot High's gymnasium was bustling with the preparations for the big spring fund-raiser. Sun splashed across the polished wooden floor. Kids were painting signs and decorating banners. The space was filled with laughter and excitement. Some of the kids were even wearing their

Canterlot Wondercolt ears and tails to show their school spirit. But what was special about the scene was how effortlessly everyone was getting along.

Jocks in team sweatshirts were chatting with the drama kids. Girls in the latest fashions shared secrets with friends in old T-shirts and jeans. It didn't seem to matter at Canterlot High what music you listened to, what clothes you wore, or what activities you did after school—everyone just seemed to be friends. Twilight Sparkle had left behind powerful magic.

But when Sunset Shimmer walked into the gym, a cloud seemed to cover the sunshine. A few kids glanced at her and turned away. One or two whispered. Sunset tried not to notice. She knew kids still didn't like her after what had happened. She *had* turned into a demonic force of evil determined to brainwash the entire student body and turn them into an army set to invade and conquer Equestria. Still, it hadn't actually happened, and she really had learned her lesson. Since then, she was trying so hard to be friendly.

Smiling, she approached Apple Bloom, Sweetie Belle, and Scootaloo, who were creating a colorful poster. None of the other girls met her eyes as she came over. Sunset sat down on the ground beside them and picked up a paintbrush dripping with red paint.

"Want some help?" she asked as sweetly as she could.

Sweetie Belle raised an eyebrow. Scootaloo covered a noise of surprise with a cough. All three girls shared a look that said, "Is she serious?"

Apple Bloom stared at Sunset coldly. "Uh, no thanks," she said. "We're good."

Disappointed, Sunset Shimmer carefully rested the paintbrush on top of the can. "Oh, okay," she said softly, glancing around the room for a friendly face.

That's when she saw Pinkie Pie waving her hands enthusiastically. "Over here, Sunset Shimmer!" she was shouting.

Immediately, Sunset skipped across the gym to where Pinkie was working with her friends Fluttershy, Rarity, Rainbow Dash, and Applejack. These were the girls who had defended Twilight Sparkle, had seen Sunset Shimmer's evil up close and personal, and yet had forgiven her the fastest.

Other kids in the gym glanced at Sunset Shimmer suspiciously as she passed. She tried to ignore the mean whispers. But she felt better when she sat down with the Equestria Girls. They were open and warm and genuine with her. It was kind of amazing, she had to admit.

"I had no idea the whole school would be here," she confided as she sat down.

Rarity held up the glittery poster she and Pinkie had been working on. All of Pinkie Pie's art projects were spectacular with sparkles!

"Quite the eye-catching advertisement, if I do say so myself." Rarity giggled. She brushed some glitter off her skirt.

"And it even smells like cake!" exclaimed Pinkie.

"It does?" said Fluttershy. She leaned close to the poster and smelled it. When she pulled her face away, it was covered in glitter and vanilla icing.

"I used vanilla frosting instead of paste!" explained Pinkie Pie, delightedly licking her fingers.

Applejack shook her head when she saw Fluttershy's glitter-covered face. "Fluttershy, you've got a little somethin'..."

Fluttershy gently wiped her cheek with her hand, brushing away a few bits of glitter. "Did I get it?" she asked.

Applejack grinned. "Not exactly!"

Sunset Shimmer giggled along with the other girls. She was happy to be included in their laughter.

Just then, a girl stood up and indignantly announced, "The Great and Powerful Trixie has run out of glue!"

She was waiting for someone to give her more glue, but none of the kids in her group responded. So Rainbow Dash leaped up, vaulted over Pinkie Pie's head, executed a perfect front handspring, and held out a bottle of glue to Trixie Lulumoon. Everyone in the room applauded Rainbow Dash's flawless floor routine—except Trixie.

"Was that really necessary?" she sneered.

"I don't know, Trixie. Is being totally excellent at everything necessary?" Rainbow Dash tossed her mane of multicolored hair and strutted back across the room to her friends. She really was good at so many different sports that sometimes she could get a little full of herself. She settled back into decorating posters as the principal walked onto a small stage at the front of the gym.

Principal Celestia was dressed in elegant purple pants and a soft beige jacket. She was young, but also smart and serious. She knew how to inspire her high school students. She cleared her throat and tapped the microphone to get everyone's attention. "Good afternoon, students!"

The kids looked up from their various projects. One boy flashed a thumbs-up, and she smiled at him.

"I just wanted to tell you," she continued, "how pleased I am that so many of you are going to participate in the first-ever Canterlot High School Musical Showcase."

Hoots and hollers of excitement roared through the gym. The kids were psyched! One kid stood up and played air guitar.

Principal Celestia beamed at her students' enthusiasm. "This is a wonderful opportunity to raise money for all our after-school programs here at Canterlot High, so keep working on those signs and posters. The more people in the community who know about the showcase, the better. I think it's going to be one of the most exciting events we've had at our school since... the Fall Formal!"

At those words, the smiles on the faces of Canterlot High's teenagers vanished. One or two kids even gasped. What a terrible, frightening night the Fall Formal had been! The battles, the zombies, the she-demon. And it had all been Sunset Shimmer's fault! Everyone was glaring at her. Well, almost everyone. Fluttershy touched her arm in support. Rarity and Rainbow Dash smiled sympathetically. Applejack winked at her, trying to let her know that all was forgiven. Pinkie Pie handed her a giant piece of construction paper, but Sunset Shimmer tried to hide behind it.

Poor Sunset Shimmer. Would anyone ever trust her again?

Music to Their Ears (and Tails!)

★ ✸ ★

The girls knew how uncomfortable it was for Sunset in the gym, so they left with her and went to the music room.

"I'm never going to live the Fall Formal down," she moaned.

"You were pretty bad." Not even Fluttershy

could defend her. She picked up her tambourine and began to shake it gently.

Sunset Shimmer slumped in a chair. "I was a demon. A raging she-demon."

Pinkie Pie hit the cymbals of her drum kit. "And you tried to turn everyone here into teenage zombies for your own personal army." Her eyes rolled back in her head, and she held out her arms stiffly, trying to make Sunset Shimmer laugh. But all Sunset Shimmer did was sink down farther in her seat.

Rarity, who had strapped on her keytar, smiled kindly at Sunset Shimmer. "Still, darling, you have us. We've forgiven you for your past…misdeeds."

The other girls all nodded in agreement as they prepped their instruments. Sunset Shimmer managed a small smile of gratitude.

"To be honest," said Applejack, who was

always honest, "I'd say the whole experience brought everyone at Canterlot High closer than ever before."

This was Pinkie's cue, and with a vibrant "One...two...three!" she executed a captivating drumroll that launched the girls into song. The Rainbooms' upbeat sounds poured out the door and through the hallways of Canterlot High, bringing with it that special magic from the land of Equestria.

The music filtered into the auditorium, where the drama kids were rehearsing the spring play. Sitting in the audience were a supportive group of soccer and lacrosse players, who gave their friends a standing ovation at the end of every scene. And then, one of Rainbow Dash's guitar solos rocked the school. Backstage, some of the tech kids who'd been fixing a broken amp high-fived one another. Off in the art studio, a stylish group of fashionistas was happily working with the Save the Environment Club to create fabulous outfits from recycled materials. One pretty girl was modeling an exotic jacket made entirely out of gum wrappers! She walked across the room like a runway model as the Rainbooms' song reached a crescendo.

As they played their instruments and sang, each of the girls began to pony up. Their long, lush tails rocked back and forth in time to the music. Their cute little ears appeared perfectly in time to the beat of the bass. Pinkie Pie went wild one last time on the drums, and exhausted, the girls harmonized with the final notes of their song. As silence returned, their pony tails and ears disappeared.

Sunset Shimmer had been watching them with a troubled mixture of joy and sadness.

She was happy to share their wonderful music, but she couldn't help wishing there was some way for her to be part of their group. Despite her confusing feelings, she clapped enthusiastically for them when they were done.

Rarity took a deep breath and exhaled. "I still can't believe that happens when we play. I have got to look into some new accessories for our band costumes. Something that looks good in a longer pony tail. Maybe some clip-on earrings for when I get those adorable pony ears."

"I just wonder *why* it happens," said Applejack, removing her bass and resting it carefully on its stand. "Princess Twilight took her crown back to Equestria. Shouldn't that mean she took all that magic back with her?"

Rainbow Dash was still strumming her guitar. She had some new riffs she wanted to try out. "Who cares *why* it happens? It makes my band totally awesome."

There was a moment of stunned silence in the music room. Fluttershy exchanged a glance with Applejack. Rarity spoke up first. "*Your* band?"

"Duh," said Rainbow Dash. She turned up her amp and began practicing some new chords. "It was my idea to start the Rainbooms so we could be in the showcase. Plus, I'm the lead guitarist."

The tiniest, almost imperceptible element of disharmony wafted through the room. What did it mean? All the girls had contributed to the band. They each had an invaluable part to play. A band was about teamwork and cooperation, after all.

Before anyone could say anything else, the handsome and dashing Flash Sentry poked his head into the music room. He had a guitar slung over his back and a wide, charming smile on his face. "Heard you outside. You guys are sounding really tight."

"We're getting there," said Rainbow Dash, her brow furrowed with worry. "Rarity's still coming in late on the second verse, and Applejack's bass solo could use a little work."

Applejack rolled her eyes. That was simply not true. Rarity looked stunned by her friend's remarks. They all helped one another improve, of course, but it was different to be critical in front of someone else, especially a boy.

As if sensing she'd gone too far, Rainbow Dash corrected herself. "They'll get it together in time for the showcase," she said.

Flash Sentry glanced around the room and coughed. "I don't suppose any of our friends from, uh, 'out of town' might come? It being a special charity event and all."

Applejack knew exactly who he was talking about, and she felt sorry for him. They all missed Twilight Sparkle, but the portal was gone and she was never coming back. And she couldn't tell Flash Sentry about the magic. "Sorry, Flash," was all she said. "I don't think Twilight's gonna be back at Canterlot High anytime soon."

He sighed with deep disappointment. "Oh. Yeah. Okay. Just, you know, thought I'd ask." He kicked at the linoleum tiles with his shoe, then shook away his very obvious heartbreak. "Keep on rockin' it," he said to the girls as he left the room.

"Well, someone is still quite the smitten kitten," said Rarity. But then she realized

Sunset was in the room. Before Twilight Sparkle had come to Canterlot High, Sunset Shimmer and Flash Sentry had been a couple. "Oh, sorry!" added Rarity. "I always forget you and Flash used to be an item."

Sunset Shimmer shrugged. "It's okay. Flash is a great guy and all, but I never really *liked* him liked him. I was just using him to become more popular."

Fluttershy gave a little gasp of surprise, and all the girls looked horrified at this.

Sunset Shimmer grimaced. "The old me really was just awful, wasn't I?"

Rarity apologized again for her insensitivity, and Rainbow Dash let Sunset know just how much the girls liked her now.

"The important thing is that you've turned yourself around," said Applejack.

And that was the truth. The girls had forgiven her, but Sunset Shimmer had also learned a lesson. She had changed.

"Thanks, Applejack," she said. "But I'm not sure everyone else at Canterlot High feels the same way."

The intercom started crackling. Someone in the office was about to make an announcement. It was Vice Principal Luna. "Sunset Shimmer, please report to the office."

"Gotta run," said Sunset Shimmer, jumping up.

The girls' faces expressed concern. Was Sunset in trouble?

"I volunteered to show some new students around the school," she explained. She grabbed her backpack. "Thought it'd be good for them to get to know the new me before they heard all the stuff about the old me."

As soon as the door shut behind her, Rainbow Dash turned back to her bandmates. "We still have a few minutes before lunch starts. Whattaya say we do 'Awesome as I Wanna Be'?" She picked up her guitar and stepped toward the microphone.

Nervously, Fluttershy pulled a notebook out of her pocket. "Um," she said softly, trying to get the attention of her friends. "Um, I was wondering if we could maybe play the song I wrote." She opened the notebook and held it up. It was covered in lightly written words and notes.

"We'll get to it," said Rainbow Dash, barely looking at it. She began strumming the beginning notes of the song she had suggested they practice.

"Oh. Okay," said Fluttershy, disappointed. She put the notebook back in her bag and picked up her tambourine. But she didn't shake it with much enthusiasm.

Rarity, too, was not playing with her usual commitment. What could possibly have happened to interfere with the girls' easy harmony?

CHAPTER

5

♥Out of Sync

✶ ✶ ✶

Sunset Shimmer practically skipped down
the hallway to the office. She was eager
to meet the new girls. Maybe they would
become her best friends. She loved the
Equestria Girls, of course. It was amazing
they were so friendly to her given everything that had happened. Still, she wasn't

really part of their group. She wasn't in the band.

She burst into the office with a big smile on her face. Three very pretty girls were standing by the secretary's desk. "Hi, are you the girls I'm supposed to show around?" she asked brightly.

Adagio Dazzle slowly turned toward her, the slightest sneer on her face. "We are," she said, without much emotion in her voice.

Sunset didn't seem to notice her disdain. "Canterlot High is a great school. You're really going to love it."

Aria Blaze snickered, and Sonata Dusk raised a single arched eyebrow.

"Oh yes," drawled Adagio Dazzle. "We really sense there's something *magical* about this place."

The three girls exchanged knowing

glances that instantly made Sunset Shimmer feel left out. Maybe these new girls weren't going to be her best friends after all, but Sunset tried not to think about that too much as she led them on a tour through the busy hallways of Canterlot. The girls followed behind her, giggling and whispering.

Sunset Shimmer took a deep breath and tried to be as friendly as she could. "That's the science lab," she said, gesturing at a door. She pointed across the hall. "The computer lab is in there."

The poster advertising the musical showcase Rarity had made in the gym was hanging on a nearby wall. "Oh, we're having a big musical showcase this weekend," explained Sunset Shimmer when she noticed the girls looking at it. "The whole school is pretty much rallying around it."

A dark and devious smile appeared on Adagio's deep red lips. "A musical showcase?"

Sunset did her best to be helpful. "I'm sure since you're new, Principal Celestia would still let you sign up if you're interested."

Aria's eyes flashed. "We have been known to sing from time to time," she said as casually as she could. Adagio grinned at her.

Sonata immediately understood the plan. "We sing, like, *all* the time. It's how we get people to do what we want!"

Adagio shot her an alarmed look. She looked like she was about to clap her hand over Sonata's mouth.

"What did I just say?" gasped Sonata Dusk.

"What you *meant* to say," interrupted Adagio Dazzle smoothly, "was that being in a musical showcase sounds like a great way to meet other students."

"Oh yeah," said Sonata, trying to recover. "I meant to say what she said. That's what I meant. To say."

Aria gave a disgusted sniff. "And what you would have said if you weren't. The. Worst."

Adagio Dazzle glared at both girls.

"You are. The. Worst." Sonata was glaring at Aria.

"Remember when I asked you for your opinion? Yeah. Me neither," answered Aria.

Noticing the alarmed expression on Sunset Shimmer's face, Adagio laughed lightly. "You'll have to excuse them. They're idiots."

Aria crossed her arms and pouted. Sonata stamped her foot and turned away.

Sunset Shimmer wasn't used to this much fighting. These days most of the kids at Canterlot High knew how to express their feelings kindly. She barely knew what to say. Trying to smooth things over, she complimented the girls on their matching necklaces. "Those are pretty," she said, reaching out her hand to the scarlet pendant dangling from around Adagio's neck. "Where did you all—"

Adagio Dazzle pulled away quickly, her wide eyes full of anger. And yet, her voice was sickeningly sweet when she spoke. "Sorry. These pendants mean an awful lot to us. We'd just hate for anything to happen to them."

Sunset immediately dropped the subject and hurried the girls to the cafeteria to finish the tour. Maybe once they were at Canterlot for a while, they would relax and learn how to be friendly. What was the matter with them? She hated to admit it to herself, but they reminded her a lot of what she had been like when she first arrived in the human realm from Equestria, in the days when popularity and power were all she had wanted.

CHAPTER

6

Devilish Divas

★ ★ ★

There were no cliques in the cafeteria at Canterlot High. It wasn't like the jocks only sat with the jocks and the brains with the brains. There were no kids sitting by themselves, unhappily chewing on their dry sandwiches. Everyone was easygoing and friendly. It was a happy place.

Sunset Shimmer was deep in thought while she waited in line for her lunch. She took a tray from Granny Smith and headed over to the table where the Rainbooms were sitting. Something was troubling her, and maybe the girls could help her figure out what it was. She sat down next to Applejack.

"How was the tour?" asked Applejack.

"I don't know. I mean, these girls, they were . . . there was something *off* about them."

"Like off like this?" Pinkie giggled. She grabbed an apple and put the whole thing in her mouth and stuck a carrot stick into either side of her hair. She spat out the apple, laughing. "Or off like this?" She grabbed two pudding cups and turned them into glasses and balanced a carrot stick like a mustache above her top lip. "Or off like…" She was grabbing for a bag of chips when Rainbow Dash stopped her.

"Maybe we just let her tell us."

Sunset shook her head and sighed. "That's just it. I can't put my finger on it. They just acted sort of strange around me…" Her voice trailed off. A terrible thought had just occurred to her. "Maybe someone had already talked to them. Told them about what I did." She sighed. "So much for making a good first impression."

Fluttershy reached out and touched her arm reassuringly. "That's probably not it." But she didn't sound very convincing.

Just then, the three new girls appeared at the cafeteria entrance. They gazed around at the happy-go-lucky students chatting and enjoying their meals.

Adagio Dazzle tossed her head. "This is it, girls. The moment we've been waiting for."

"Lunch!" said Sonata Dusk with confidence.

Adagio sneered. "The chance to get our true Equestrian magic back."

"Oh. Right."

"Our voices are just strong enough to make them want something so badly they'll fight to get it," hissed Adagio.

"So we're just going to do what we always do?" questioned Aria, her voice dripping with boredom. "Stir up some trouble and then feed off the negative energy? Some plan, Adagio."

"It won't be the same as the times before," said Adagio Dazzle fiercely. "There is Equestrian magic here. *Their* negative energy will give us the power we need to get this entire world to do our bidding."

Sonata bit her lip as she tried to understand. "But we can get lunch after, though, right? It's Taco Tuesday."

Adagio let out an irritated groan. "Just follow my lead!"

"Or my lead!" announced Aria.

"*My* lead," said Adagio firmly.

Aria pouted as Adagio pursed her lips and began to hum. At first, it was quiet, but slowly her voice became louder, her tune more intoxicating. Aria began to harmonize with her, and eventually Sonata stopped sulking and also joined in.

Kids began to turn toward the music. When all eyes were on them, the girls burst into full song. Their a cappella number was riveting. *"Never wanted anything more!"* they serenaded the school. The Canterlot High students were captivated by these new girls. They were extraordinary.

Applause echoed through the cafeteria as the girls took their bows. Adagio used this moment center stage to make an announcement. Smiling sweetly, she let everyone know how thrilled she was to participate in the showcase, but wouldn't it be so much more fun if, instead of a showcase, it was a competition?

"Wouldn't this be a wonderful...opportunity," she enthused, "to determine who is the very best band at Canterlot High? What this school needs is a Battle of the Bands!"

Adagio raised her arms over her head triumphantly, like she was expecting more applause. But the room was strangely silent. Kids were shaking their heads, conferring with one another, and deciding they didn't like the idea at all. Not one bit.

But Adagio Dazzle and her friends began singing again, and as their entrancing music filled the room, their scarlet pendants began to glow. The girls spread out, weaving from table to table through the cafeteria, and slowly the protests dwindled as the students were swept up in the enchantment of the song.

Soon, kids were announcing that they'd always wanted a Battle of the Bands at Canterlot High. One group of kids decided they were going to do whatever it took to win the competition.

"We're going to be the best band," announced some girls at a table.

"No, we are," said some boys from across the room.

Everyone was arguing now, determined to win the upcoming battle. Everyone, that is, except the Sonic Rainbooms and Sunset Shimmer. They sat at their table in a state of stunned silence. What was happening to the harmony of Canterlot High? Where had it gone?

Pinkie remembered what Sunset had said about the girls. Now she got it. "Oooh," she exclaimed. "Those girls are *that* kind of 'off.' "

Facing the Music

✶ ✶ ✶

Sunset Shimmer, Rainbow Dash, Rarity, Fluttershy, Pinkie Pie, and Applejack hurried down the hall toward the principal's office. They had to talk to her right away!

"Those three are definitely in possession of some kind of dark magic," said Sunset breathlessly. "How else could you explain what happened back there?"

"Don't worry, y'all," said Applejack. "We'll let Principal Celestia know about this, and those girls'll be kicked to the curb in no time. Last thing she needs is another Canterlot High event almost ruined by some power-crazed lunatic."

The girls all stopped, stunned.

"No offense," said Applejack to Sunset Shimmer.

Sunset Shimmer sighed. "None taken." Well, she might never live down the catastrophe of the Fall Formal, but at least she could stop another one from happening.

Principal Celestia and Vice Principal Luna welcomed the girls and invited them to sit down. But they were too agitated. All talking at once, they tried to explain to them what had happened in the cafeteria with the new girls.

"Dark magic?" questioned Principal Celestia. "I find that very hard to believe. Those girls came into my office earlier and were absolutely delightful."

Vice Principal Luna agreed and then cleared her throat. She looked very stern as she stared at Sunset. "Perhaps Sunset Shimmer is just eager to make someone else out to be a bad element here at Canterlot High, so her actions at the Fall Formal will become old news."

Sunset Shimmer felt a cold weight in her stomach. If only everyone would let go of that. "I can see why you might think so," she said, trying to behave responsibly. "But—"

"That's not what's happening now,"

interrupted Rainbow Dash. "We saw all of this go down in the cafeteria, too."

Principal Celestia crossed her arms and looked thoughtful. "Yes, but isn't *your* band supposed to be part of the musical showcase?"

"Yes," said Rainbow Dash, not sure where this was going.

Principal Celestia and Vice Principal Luna exchanged a knowing glance.

"Perhaps you're all just worried that the Dazzlings will steal your spotlight," said Vice Principal Luna gently.

"The Dazzlings?" Applejack burst out.

"It's the name of their musical group," explained Principal Celestia. "That's why they came by my office earlier—to sign up for the showcase. Even sang a little song to Vice Principal Luna and me." She smiled at the memory of it, but her eyes went a little blank.

The girls noticed it instantly.

"They did?" asked Applejack. She was beginning to notice a pattern.

"Yes," said Principal Celestia. "And we think having a Battle of the Bands instead of a show-case is a marvelous idea. In fact…"

"We've never wanted anything more," said Principal Celestia and Vice Principal Luna together, almost robotically, like they'd been programmed to speak that way.

The girls exchanged worried glances. They knew instantly that they were on their own. They excused themselves as quickly as they could and gathered at the Wondercolt statue in front of the school. It felt good to be outside in the fresh air and away from the strange magic that was invisibly permeating their beloved Canterlot High.

Fluttershy looked like she was on the edge of tears. "I can't believe they got to Principal Celestia and Vice Principal Luna, too."

Rainbow Dash shook her head. "They've gotten to everybody."

"Not everybody," announced Pinkie Pie with determination.

Applejack nodded. "Pinkie Pie's right. We were there when the Dazzlings were singing, and we weren't affected. It was like we were protected somehow."

"So let's take the Dazzlings down!" exclaimed Rainbow Dash, her hands on her hips, ready for a fight. "It's not like we haven't tangled with dark magic before and totally whopped its sorry butt." She glanced at Sunset Shimmer. "Uh, no offense."

Sunset almost laughed. She was getting so used to it. "None taken. Again."

Fluttershy was looking increasingly concerned. "But that was when Twilight was here. There may be some kind of magic inside us, but it only comes out when we play music. I sure don't know how to use it to whop anybody's butt."

Rarity had been gazing at the statue where so many of last fall's events had taken place. It had been the magic portal between this world and Equestria, and now it was closed forever. "If only we could get a message to her. Maybe she could tell us how to break the spell the Dazzlings have cast on our friends."

Rainbow Dash slapped her hand against the solid base of the statue. "Well, that's not gonna happen. I get the feeling they don't exactly have cell phones where she's from."

But Sunset Shimmer was actually from Equestria, even if her time there felt like a distant dream. Suddenly, she was struck by an idea. "I may have a way we can get in touch with Princess Twilight!"

Immediately, she began running toward the school lot where her car was parked. The other girls followed quickly behind her, wondering what she could be up to. Sunset Shimmer had opened her trunk and was rummaging around inside, looking for something.

"When I was Princess Celestia's student back in Equestria," she explained, "she gave me...THIS!" She held up a book. On the cover was Princess Celestia's cutie mark.

The other girls looked at it with wonder, not sure what this meant, but Sunset Shimmer was bubbling with excitement. "Even after I abandoned my studies, I held on to it. Deep down I guess I knew I was making a big mistake and wanted to still have a way to reach out to her."

Sunset flipped open the book, revealing several pages of elaborate cursive writing. She stopped at an empty page. She beamed at the other girls, her eyes wide. "Maybe it still works!"

"It's a book, darling," said Rarity as sweetly as she could. "What do you mean 'Maybe it still works'?"

"It used to be that if I wrote something in here, it would appear in the pages of a book back in Princess Celestia's library." She took a big breath. She could barely contain her anticipation. "I get a message to her, then she can get a message to Princess Twilight."

The girls exploded with squeals! There

was a way to get in touch with Twilight Sparkle after all.

"So what are you waiting for?" demanded Rainbow Dash. "Get to writing!" She pulled a pen out of her pocket and handed it to Sunset Shimmer.

The girls crowded around as Sunset stared at the empty page of the book. The girls at Canterlot had forgiven her, but she wasn't sure that Twilight Sparkle had. The girls were smiling at her, and it gave her confidence. "Been a long time since I've written these words," she gulped. "'Dear Princess Celestia...'"

As Sunset Shimmer continued writing, white light began to flash and a swirl of sparkling rainbows erupted from the book.

CHAPTER

8

In the Key of Princess

★ ★ ★

Far away in Equestria, Twilight Sparkle was moving into a castle befitting her new status as a princess. All her favorite pony friends were helping her get settled. Even now, they still reminded her of their teenage counterparts in the human world. She had told them all so many stories about her adventures at Canterlot High.

Her thoughts were interrupted by Rarity. "Why, Twilight, it must be quite overwhelming, moving from a one-bedroom loft to such an expansive home. You will give me a chance to help decorate the place, won't you?"

Princess Twilight teased her friend. "I'll think about it." But Rarity was so instantly devastated that the royalty rushed to reassure her. "I'm kidding. Of course you can."

Applejack was laughing. "Who-ee! You shoulda seen your face, Rarity!"

Princess Twilight threw open the heavy doors to the throne room. Her assistant, Spike the dragon, had dragged a huge canvas mailbag across the room and was dumping it out next to an already enormous pile of letters. "More mail for the Princess of Friendship," the dragon explained.

Pinkie Pie squealed, took a flying leap, and dived into the letters like it was a pile of leaves. She emerged a moment later, enthusiastically reading some of the return addresses on Princess Twilight's fan mail. "From Maretonia, Appleloosa, Vanhoover…"

"Gosh," exclaimed Fluttershy. "Who knew there were so many ponies in need of your services?"

Rainbow Dash whinnied in agreement. "Seriously, is there anypony in Equestria who isn't looking for you to solve their problems?"

Princess Twilight suddenly looked very serious. "I am the Princess of Friendship now, and it is my job to have the answers.

And I've already got Spike categorizing the issues according to urgency." Her friends were going to have to understand that being princess wasn't just about balls and tiaras—it was a lot of responsibility.

Applejack understood that. "Course you do."

Spike ripped open one of the letters. "Here's a good one. Somepony in Manehattan says he bought a big salad for a friend and another friend took credit for it. Wants to know what to do."

Rarity laughed. "I'd say that one can go in the not-so-urgent pile."

A delivery pony knocked politely on the open door. He was carrying a large box. "Excuse me, Princess, where do you want all these books from Princess Celestia?"

"The library," answered Princess Twilight. She gestured to a door that led out of the throne room. "It's down that hallway."

"Should I bring them all there? Even this one that's glowin' and vibratin'?"

Princess Twilight raised her eyebrows, intrigued. With a delicate wave of magic, she summoned the mysterious book from the box. On the cover was emblazoned Sunset Shimmer's cutie mark! How surprising! What could this mean?

She opened the book carefully and watched as cursive lettering began to magically appear on the pages.

"What is it?" asked Fluttershy, leaning in for a better look.

Twilight Sparkle could barely speak, she was so amazed. "It looks like...a message to Princess Celestia...from my friends at Canterlot High."

The other ponies crowded around to examine the words.

Rarity shook her head. Twilight Sparkle had explained to them that the portal to the other world was closed forever. "How is that even possible?"

"I have no idea," answered Twilight Sparkle, mystified. "But…" And she took a deep breath filled with grave concern for her human friends. "It sounds like they need my help!"

Her pony friends watched as she studied the message for a long time and then galloped down the hallway to the library. They followed and discovered her pulling books off the shelves and out of boxes. "The way Sunset Shimmer describes them, I think these new girls sound an awful lot like the Sirens."

"Not the Sirens!" gasped Pinkie Pie. She whispered to the other ponies, "I don't actually know who that is."

Twilight Sparkle found the book she was looking for and placed it, open, on the table. "The Sirens were three beautiful but dangerous creatures who had the power to charm ponies with their music," she explained. She showed the other ponies a detailed drawing of three beautiful spirit-like creatures with wings on their backs and talons where their hooves should be. Their mouths were open, and they were clearly singing. Around their necks, they each wore a pendant with a scarlet jewel.

" 'To maintain this power, they fed on the negativity and distrust of others. The more of this negative energy they consumed, the stronger their voices became and the farther they could spread their dark magic,'" Twilight read. She turned the page.

There was a picture of the Sirens levitating over a group of arguing ponies. Their mouths were open, and their pendants glowed. The ponies in the picture looked angry and unhappy, and the Sirens looked triumphant.

Fluttershy shivered. "I don't think I like this story very much."

"'If the Sirens had gotten their way, they would have divided and conquered all of Equestria,'" explained Twilight Sparkle, reading more. "'But a certain Star Swirl the Bearded wasn't having it.'"

Twilight grinned as she held the book up to show the ponies a picture of Star Swirl the Bearded. "'Rumor has it, he found a way to banish them to another world. One where he believed their magical power would be lost forever.'"

The smile vanished from Twilight Sparkle's face as she realized exactly what world that was. "That world must have been the one where my Canterlot High friends live."

"But Star Swirl must've sent them there moons ago. How come they're just surfacin' now?" asked Applejack, rubbing her head.

"I don't know," answered Twilight, but she was very worried. "If my hunch is right and it is the Sirens who've come to Canterlot High, this spell they've cast is just the beginning." Twilight was resolved. Being a princess meant helping others, and this was certainly more important than settling a fight about salads. "My friends need me. I have to get back to them."

"Hate to burst your bubble, Twilight," said Rainbow Dash. "But the mirror you used to get to Canterlot High doesn't work anymore. The connection between their world and Equestria has been totally cut off for another thirty moons."

"Okay," said Pinkie Pie, interrupting. "First of all, if there was bubble blowing going on, why wasn't I told about it? And second, if the connection is *totally* cut off, how was Sunset Shimmer able to get that message to Twilight?" With her usual slapdash excitement, Pinkie Pie had hit the nail on the head!

"Pinkie Pie, you're a genius!" Twilight gave her a hug.

"Yeah. I get that a lot." Pinkie Pie grinned, trying to be nonchalant. "Now about those bubbles..."

Rainbow Road Trip

✶ ✶ ✶

Princess Twilight Sparkle had been very busy assembling a complicated contraption that connected Princess Celestia's book at one end to the no-longer-working portal mirror on the other end. She was trying to explain it to her friends, who were looking on in amazement. "...and the interval between the two points is defined as the square root of the sum of the squares of the separation between the points along the three spatial dimensions."

Spike shook his head. "Say what now?"

"Duh," said Pinkie Pie, who didn't understand what was so confusing. She pointed at the book. "She's gonna take the magic in here and put it in there." With a flourish, she gestured to the mirror. "That will make the portal open up so that whenever she wants to, she can go from here to there. There to here. Here to there. There to here. Here to there. There to—"

"We get the idea," interrupted Applejack.

"Now to see if it actually works!" Twilight pulled a lever and sparks immediately burst from the book and sent an electrical charge into the machine that slowly began making its way toward the mirror.

"Ooooh!"

"Ahhh!"

"Wow!"

The portal mirror was beginning to shimmer and glow!

Carefully, Twilight approached the mirror to test it. She placed her hoof on its reflective surface—and her hoof disappeared! She pulled it back. The machine was going to work!

"Don't suppose we could join you this time around?" asked Applejack.

Twilight Sparkle shook her head. "Better not. It could make things confusing in Canterlot High if all of a sudden there were two of all of you."

The ponies nodded in understanding.

"But I still get to go, right?" piped up Spike. "There isn't another one of me at Canterlot High. And you never know when you might need your trusty assistant."

Twilight smiled at her friend and held out her hand. Spike pumped his fist before taking it. "We won't be gone long," she said.

The girls hugged one another, and each of the ponies whispered special words of encouragement to the princess. They hoped she was up to defeating the Sirens. It was scary having her leave their world again.

"Ready, Spike?" asked Twilight Sparkle at last.

"Ready!"

The two stepped into the mirror together. Almost instantly, there was a flash of blinding white light. Streaks of rainbow colors blazed in all directions as Twilight and Spike were stretched and squashed and bent and transformed into another dimension. Sparks glittered in the throne room in Equestria. At the marble base of the Wondercolt statue, tiny, almost imperceptible rainbows began to emerge.

The human girls had been waiting and waiting since Sunset Shimmer sent her message. They were beginning to lose hope. Rainbow Dash kept wishing they would see something, anything. She studied the statue one last time and was about to suggest they give up when Twilight Sparkle, the teenage girl, and Spike, her pet dog, flew out of the portal and hit the ground with an enormous thud!

"Twilight!" shouted all the girls, rushing

to their long-lost friend. There were hugs and squeals and tears.

Twilight was wobbly and a little bruised. "I'm back!" She dusted herself off. It wasn't quite the entrance she had imagined making. Still, she'd made it, and that's what mattered. "I've got some bad news about those new girls," she said, almost at once. She noticed the worried glances her friends were exchanging. She hoped that it wasn't too late.

CHAPTER

10

Reunion
Rhythms

★ ★ ★

There was so much to catch up on, and the best place to do that was at the Sweet Shoppe. Pinkie Pie brought Twilight Sparkle a giant hot chocolate with lots of whipped cream.

Everyone was talking all at once.

Rarity wished that they could all just

chat about fun things. "Oh, I do so hate that you've had to return in a time of crisis. We have so much to tell you!"

"For starters, a certain blue-haired guitar player was just asking about you," announced Applejack forthrightly.

A giddy smile lit up Twilight's face. "Flash Sentry was asking about me?" Immediately, she tried to play it cool. She blew on her hot chocolate to hide her excitement. "Isn't that nice."

"Perhaps you could give us just the slightest bit of gossip from your world," said Rarity.

"She's got an official title now," whispered Spike. He had to make sure no one else heard the talking dog and got alarmed. "She's the Princess of Friendship!" He mimed blowing a royal trumpet.

"Wow! That's really impressive," said Sunset

Shimmer with absolute sincerity. "Guess you really were Princess Celestia's prized pupil."

"She even got her own castle," bragged Spike.

Rarity hugged Twilight with excitement. "A castle?! You have your own castle!" In her excitement, she spilled the hot chocolate. Rarity grabbed a napkin and began mopping at her friend's shirt. "How lovely," she said, trying to behave more coolly. Still, it wasn't every day you find out your friend has her very own castle!

"What's new here?" asked Twilight. "I mean, besides your school becoming the target of dangerous magical creatures from Equestria."

Rainbow Dash exchanged a worried glance with the other girls. They all nodded their heads. They wanted her to tell Twilight.

"Yeah," began Rainbow Dash. "So that isn't exactly the *first* strange thing that's happened since you left." She took out her cell phone and showed Twilight Sparkle videos of each of the girls playing music—and ponying up. "Pretty sweet, huh? Happens to all of us when we play."

Twilight took the phone from Rainbow Dash and studied the videos. This explained a lot. In fact, it explained *everything* about the Sirens—and what to do about them. "My crown was returned to Equestria, but some of its magic must have remained here at Canterlot High. Now that we're all back together, we can use that magic on the Sirens. Just like we were able to use it on Sunset Shimmer when she turned into that horrifyingly awful winged monster." Twilight Sparkle clapped her hand over her mouth.

She remembered too late that Sunset was sitting with them. "No offense," she apologized.

"None taken." Sunset sighed. "I'm used to it."

"They'll never even know what hit 'em," said Rainbow Dash, returning to the topic of the Sirens. She executed some bold karate moves.

Applejack leaned back, more relaxed than she'd been since the Sirens started singing. "We've got nothin' to worry about now that Twilight's back."

"Oh, I'm pretty sure I could find something to worry about," said Fluttershy, suddenly overwhelmed by a hundred and one different things. But then she looked at Twilight Sparkle's confident face. "But it won't be the Sirens," she added brightly.

Twilight Sparkle knew the girls were

counting on her. "The sooner we do this the better. Any idea where the Sirens might be?" she asked.

"There's a big party tonight at the gym for all the bands who signed up to be in the showcase," gushed Pinkie Pie, who always knew where every party was. "That would include the Dazzlings, the band the Sirens have formed."

"Looks like we've got a party to crash," resolved Twilight Sparkle grimly. The girls would have to finish getting caught up later—when Canterlot High was no longer in danger.

The girls gulped down their drinks, piled into Sunset Shimmer's car, and headed to the gym. The moment they entered, however, they could tell that something was the matter. Something serious. This was no party.

Small groups of kids were huddled

together, whispering among one another. They were shooting competitive stares at others in the group. The energy in the room was tense, unhappy, and mean.

Flash Sentry, looking grim and miserable, broke away from his bandmates and was just heading to get more punch when he ran right into Twilight Sparkle. She nearly toppled over with surprise, but he expertly wrapped his arm around her and pulled her back up, like it was a move in a dance.

Twilight was blushing. "Bumped. Into. Always. Doing . . ." She could barely talk.

"Twilight?!" exclaimed Flash Sentry. "What are you doing here? You came back for the big competition, right? I knew you would!"

Twilight smiled up at him. He was even handsomer than she remembered. "Something like that."

Flash looked determined. "Not that there's going to be any *real* competition. No one here wants this as bad as my band does."

His competitiveness alarmed Twilight Sparkle, and just at that moment, she spotted three girls with sneers on their pretty faces entering the gym. Those were the Sirens. She was sure of it.

"Can you excuse me for just a minute?" she said to Flash. She motioned to her friends to follow her.

Adagio Dazzle was looking around the gym at the students divided into tight little cliques. "Oh no!" she said with mock sincerity. "No one's mingling. It's like there's some kind of underlying tension that could bubble to the surface at any minute." She laughed wickedly.

"It's the fruit punch, isn't it? I knew I

used too much grape juice." Sonata Dusk held up an empty juice bottle.

Adagio gave an exasperated sigh. "It's not the fruit punch. It's *us*," she explained.

"But the punch is awful, too," Aria Blaze noted.

"What do you know about good fruit punch?" Sonata spat.

"More than you," shot back Aria.

"Do not."

"Do, too."

Adagio ignored their bickering and focused on the partygoers. "This is just the kickoff party," she said to herself. "Imagine what a tizzy they'll be in by the time the Battle of the Bands starts."

Right behind her, in a loud, clear voice, Twilight Sparkle announced, "There isn't going to be a Battle of the Bands! We're going to make sure of it!"

Everyone stopped talking. The room was hushed.

"All right, girls. Let's do this!" shouted Twilight to her friends.

The girls clasped hands and waited for the rainbow magic that always came when they were together with Twilight Sparkle. But this time nothing happened. They waited another beat. Still, nothing. The crowd was staring at them, and the Equestria Girls were just standing there holding hands with their eyes closed. Rainbow Dash peeked out at the gym.

"Um, weren't there rainbows and lasers and stuff last time?" she whispered to the other girls.

"I don't understand," said Twilight Sparkle. "We're all together again. Why isn't this working? This is all we had to do last time to defeat Sunset Shimmer. We just had to come together and hold hands."

From a backpack over in the corner, Spike popped out his head. "You really need to go ahead and do that whole Magic of Friendship thing now," he whispered as quietly as he could to Twilight Sparkle.

"I'm trying, Spike," she said under her breath. "I thought the six of us standing together against the Sirens would bring out the magic we needed to defeat them. That's what happened before."

Adagio seized the moment. "Talk about throwing down the gauntlet! This group is obviously serious about winning," she said to the gathered teens. "A little cocky, though, aren't they? Claiming there won't really be a battle. Seems they think they've already got this thing all locked up."

Trixie stepped out from the crowd with her band of girls in a tight formation behind her. "Not if the Great and Powerful Trixie has anything to do with it."

Flash faced off against Trixie. "Whatever, Trixie. We're the best band at Canterlot High. We're the ones who'll be going the distance." Their faces were silhouetted by the faintest of sickly green lights.

They began arguing about which band was better. The Cutie Mark Crusaders insisted they were the best band. Snips and Snails yelled at them and insisted they were going to win. Everyone was shouting and fighting and squabbling. Every new quarrel seemed to produce another thread of green light. Adagio, Aria, and Sonata smiled contentedly as their scarlet pendants absorbed it and seemed to grow brighter.

Twilight Sparkle noticed what was happening and was more worried than ever. She gestured to her friends to leave the room, while they still could.

Adagio watched them go with a sinister smile. "I think we may have found what we're looking for. Or rather, it found us."

Sonata stared at her blankly.

Adagio nearly screamed in frustration. "Magic! Don't you see? Don't you see? Everyone else has fallen under our spell. But not these girls. These girls are special. And they've got exactly what we need to grow more powerful than ever!"

The Band to Beat

★ ★ ★

Out in the parking lot, Twilight Sparkle was beside herself. The Equestria Girls were all looking at her expectantly, but she couldn't figure out why the magic hadn't worked. "It doesn't make any sense," she said, pacing back and forth. "I should have been able to create the spark that would help us break their spell. That's how it worked before."

Sunset Shimmer had been thinking about that night, too. "To defeat me, you drew magic from the crown I was wearing," she remembered. "I had used it to create dark magic, and you used it to help create the Magic of Friendship." She stopped. She realized something. She had figured it out! "The Sirens' magic comes from their music. So maybe you have to use the same kind of magic to defeat them."

Twilight stopped pacing and stared at Sunset.

"Or maybe not," said Sunset, suddenly self-conscious.

"No. I think you're onto something."

"Really?" said Sunset, brightening.

Twilight turned to the other girls. "It's when you play music that you transform now, right? When the magic inside you comes out?"

"Yep," said Applejack. "Ears. Tails. The whole shebang."

Twilight was looking much happier. "So maybe the way to use that magic to defeat the Sirens is by playing a musical counterspell."

"You mean like a song?" asked Fluttershy.

Twilight nodded. "And in order to free everyone who's been exposed to the Sirens' spell, we'll need them all to hear it."

The girls thought about this for a moment, and then Rarity realized the perfect way to do that. "The band competition! That's the next time we can be certain everyone will be in the same place at the same time."

Applejack slapped her thigh. "Guess the Rainbooms *are* the band to beat at the Battle of the Bands!"

"And I know who the newest member of the Rainbooms is," beamed Rainbow. "It's you, Twilight!"

All the girls were so happy—except for Sunset Shimmer, who stepped aside into the shadows so the girls could all enjoy their reunion. It looked like a lot of fun to be in a band.

Pinkie Pie was brimming with ideas for what instrument Twilight Sparkle should play. "Triangle? Sousaphone? Theremin?" she suggested. "Soooooo magical!"

Twilight laughed. "It might take a little too long to learn how to play some of those.... I'll just sing."

Rainbow Dash looked confused. "Like,

as lead singer? 'Cause that's usually *my* gig. This being my band and all."

"It's *our* band," corrected Applejack. "And of course Twilight Sparkle will be lead singer. She's the one with the magical know-how to help us pull this thing off."

Rainbow Dash exhaled slowly, taking in the news. "Okay. Yeah. That's cool." She tossed her hair. She was used to being the most valuable player on the team, it was true, and it was hard for her to let go of that. "I'll just use this as a chance to hone my already insanely good lead guitar skills."

Applejack rolled her eyes.

"It's only temporary," said Twilight Sparkle, stepping in. "And we don't have to win the Battle of the Bands. We just have to perform the counterspell during the first round of the competition." There was entirely enough rivalry making everyone unhappy at Canterlot High.

"So let's get to learning that musical counterspell," said Rainbow Dash, rediscovering her team spirit.

"That's just it. I don't know any," admitted Twilight Sparkle.

The girls' shoulders slumped with disappointment.

"But I could figure out how to write one," suggested Twilight Sparkle. She would not let her friends down. She was a magical pony princess, after all.

"Totally!" chimed in Spike. "Twilight can write a spell like nobody's business. That's pretty much how she got to become royalty in Equestria."

"Technically I helped finish a spell," she

explained. "And there was a little more to it than that, Spike."

"Yeah. Whatever." He winked at the girls. "Twilight's totally got this."

Their eyes wide and hopeful, they all looked at Twilight.

"I've got this," she said confidently. "Come on, Spike." The two headed back through the darkness toward the high school.

"Where you goin'?" shouted Applejack after them.

"Last time we were here, Spike and I slept in the library."

"Are you crazy?!" said Pinkie Pie. "We're besties now! You're staying at my house. It's time for a slumber party!"

Pajama Jam

✦ ✦ ✦

Pinkie Pie's bedroom was decorated all in pink. The walls were pink; her desk was pink. Her bed had pink pillows and a pink comforter. And the pajamas she had given to Twilight Sparkle to wear were soft and fuzzy and, of course, pink.

Twilight was sitting on Pinkie Pie's bed

deep in thought. She had a notebook Fluttershy had given her in her lap. She was humming softly to herself, trying out tunes and lyrics and writing them down. She had to find just the right words and melody to counteract the spell.

Rainbow Dash and Applejack, also in their pajamas, were playing a video game together. Pinkie Pie was checking out gossip on her computer. "Status update: Okeydokey-lokey!"

Rarity held up her phone and took a selfie with Sunset Shimmer and Fluttershy in the picture. "Gorgeous!" she said, checking it out.

Sunset was smiling happily in the photo. It felt good to be included. How could she have ever thought being an all-powerful, all-lonely she-demon would be more fun than this? If only the Sirens could understand that, but Twilight would have to defeat them first.

Rainbow Dash turned off the video game.

"Hey! I was about to beat you!" exclaimed Applejack.

"I doubt it," bragged Rainbow Dash. "Hey, Twilight, how's the counterspell coming?"

Twilight stopped humming and looked up. "Huh? Oh, uh, good. Great," she said distractedly. "Thanks for letting me use your notebook, Fluttershy." She flipped to an earlier page in the book covered in Fluttershy's writing. "I really like the song you wrote for the Rainbooms."

Fluttershy blushed. "Thanks." Then she

added so softly that only Twilight heard her, "Hopefully one day we'll get a chance to play it."

Rarity plopped down on the bed next to Twilight Sparkle. "Dearest Twilight, I think I speak for all of us when I say that I don't know what we would have done if you hadn't been able to come back and help us."

All the girls chimed in, agreeing with her. Without Twilight Sparkle, there would be no hope against the Sirens! A doorbell ringing downstairs interrupted them.

"Pizza's here!" announced Pinkie Pie, jumping up. The girls all dashed downstairs. All except for Twilight Sparkle.

Everyone had such faith in her, but she just couldn't come up with the right words. She picked up the notebook and studied it again. The page where she had been working was blank except for a single line, which had been crossed out. What was she going to do?

Pinkie Pie poked her head back into the bedroom. "Don't you want any pizza?"

Twilight nodded and followed Pinkie downstairs, but not before tucking the notebook under a pillow.

Late that night, after all the girls had finally stopped giggling and fallen asleep, Twilight slipped out of her sleeping bag, tiptoed around the girls, and retrieved the notebook. Quietly, she made her way downstairs to the kitchen. She had to come up with a solution before the girls woke up!

She scribbled down words and phrases and crossed them out. She chewed on the end of her pen. "No, that's not going to work," she said to herself. She wrote down something else and stared at it, dissatisfied.

A gentle voice interrupted her work. "Hey, Twilight," said Sunset Shimmer, coming into the kitchen.

Twilight nearly jumped out of her skin with surprise! She dropped her pen.

"You're up late," noted Sunset, sitting down at the table with her.

"Just looking over the counterspell. We only get one shot at this. It has to be perfect." Casually, she closed the notebook so Sunset couldn't see how little she'd actually written.

"We really are lucky you're here," said Sunset.

"That's what everyone keeps telling me." Twilight sighed.

There had been so much Sunset Shimmer had wanted to say to Twilight Sparkle after the disastrous events of last fall, and no time to say it before she had disappeared, seemingly forever. Sunset noticed the worried look on Twilight's face. She got up and opened the door to the fridge, and laughed when she saw its contents. "Who could possibly need this much whipped cream?"

She began moving canisters of the topping around, looking for a healthier midnight snack. "Must be nice to have everyone always looking to you for answers," she said to Twilight from inside the fridge. "Instead of waiting for you to cause a problem."

But Twilight felt just as blue as Sunset Shimmer. Maybe Princess Celestia had made a mistake. Maybe she wasn't cut out to be a magical princess. "Just because everyone expects something from you, doesn't mean it's guaranteed to happen," she confided.

"But that doesn't stop them from expecting it," noted Sunset.

"Which only makes things harder because the last thing you want to do is—"

"Let everybody down!" said both girls at the same time.

Sunset turned around and stared at Twilight. Maybe the two of them had more in common than she thought. Being a good friend wasn't always easy; that's what she was discovering. It was a lot of responsibility.

A figure with arms outstretched, holding a rock in her open palm, staggered into the kitchen. It was Maud Pie! "Boulder was hungry," she said, her voice flat and dull. It was always a surprise to the girls that the vibrant Pinkie Pie had such a lackluster older sister.

Sunset Shimmer and Twilight watched

silently as Maud walked over to the pantry and grabbed a box of crackers.

"I still can't get over the fact that she's related to Pinkie Pie," Sunset Shimmer whispered to Twilight.

"You and me both."

Maud had opened the crackers and was crumbling them over Boulder in a kind of daze. She reached in for another handful. Clearly, she was going to go through the entire box before she was done. She explained that she was feeding her pet rock.

"Better get some sleep," said Sunset Shimmer. "Good luck with the counterspell. Not that you'll need it. This must be nothing compared to the stuff you're expected to deal with as a princess in Equestria."

"But what if I can't..." began Twilight, ready to share her doubts and worries, but

Sunset had already headed back upstairs. She opened her notebook again with a deep sigh. "No. I have to be able to do this. I have to."

She began humming and writing again while beside her Maud Pie "fed" Boulder more crumbled crackers. But as she worked, she felt more and more hopeless. What would happen to Canterlot High if she couldn't come up with a counterspell? She could barely think about it, but she knew that she could never return to Equestria as a princess if she couldn't take care of her friends right here, right now.

Princess in Peril

★ ★ ★

The Rainbooms gathered together at Apple-jack's Sweet Apple Acres Co-op the next day, setting up their instruments in the barn to practice. Sunset Shimmer and Spike were sitting together to watch the rehearsal, but Spike kept covering his ears. The music was terrible! The girls were trying to play the song Twilight had written, but they couldn't seem to blend their instruments, find the right rhythms, or even sing in tune. Even worse, they would start to pony up and then stop halfway as if something was terribly the matter.

Rarity got a tail but not ears. Fluttershy grew wings, but no one else did. One ear popped out of Pinkie Pie's head but not both. Rainbow Dash's mane kept growing and growing until it wrapped around her guitar and made it impossible to play!

"I think it's pretty obvious what's going wrong with this counterspell," said Rainbow Dash over the cacophony of the music.

"You're turning what should be the chorus into a five-minute guitar solo?" Applejack criticized. She was getting tired of Rainbow Dash's need to always be the star.

"I have to pick up the slack somehow. Are you guys even trying?" Rainbow Dash tried to untangle her mane from the guitar.

"I'm trying," said Fluttershy softly.

Big Mac, Applejack's older brother, poked his head into the barn. Almost immediately, he ducked back out of the room, covering his ears with his hands just like Spike. The Rainbooms put down their instruments, and silence filled the barn at last. Spike and Sunset looked relieved.

Spike tried to be supportive, but he wasn't very convincing. "That sounded way better than the last five times you played it."

Twilight Sparkle was frazzled. She hadn't slept all night, and now one of her eyes was twitching. "It's fine. It will be fine," she said to herself. Taking a deep breath, she turned toward the other girls. "One more time from the top."

Rarity spoke up first. "Or perhaps we should take a short break? Try on some of the wardrobe choices I've put together?" She ran over to a rack of clothing in the barn, riffled through it, and produced a bright blue rock-and-roll jacket like something the Running Hooves would have worn in their heyday. "I'm particularly fond of this one. Of course we could always go with something a bit more modern...."

"We're tryin' to save our school here. Enough with the costumes," said Applejack, fiddling with her amp. She kept getting all kinds of screeching feedback when she tried to play.

Rarity was trying on more outfits, and now she was dressed in black leather with a metallic neon-lit helmet, like she was in Mad Steed. "You can never have enough costumes," she said in a strange electronic voice.

"Rarity just wants to make things fun," said Pinkie Pie supportively. "Isn't that what being in a band is supposed to be about?"

Sunset Shimmer shook her head. "Hate to be the bearer of bad news, guys, but you don't have time for any of this. You're supposed to check in at the Battle of the Bands in fifteen minutes."

The girls went nuts. They had completely lost track of time. The whole day had vanished while they struggled to play Twilight's song. Now they had to pack up their instruments. There was no more time to practice.

The next time they played the song, they would be performing it.

Twilight Sparkle was clearly panicked. "But...but it's not ready. If we play the counterspell in the first round and it doesn't work, the Sirens will know what we're up to and make sure we don't get a chance to play it again."

Applejack was practical as always. "Then we'll have to buy ourselves some time so you can keep workin' on it."

"And how do you propose we do that?" asked Rarity. The song wasn't ready. Their costumes weren't ready. This was a mess!

But Rainbow Dash didn't think so. She had a plan. "We compete in the Battle of the Bands for real. I take over lead vocals again, and we stay alive until the finals. We unleash the counterspell then." She turned to Twilight. "You'll have it figured out by the finals, right?"

"Of course she will," said Spike, jumping in. "Twilight Sparkle's never met a problem she couldn't solve. Right, Twilight?"

Twilight tried to smile, but her eyes were filled with anxiety. "Right."

Rainbow Dash had the fighting spirit, though. She knew she was a great singer, a lead singer. She won every game she played in, didn't she? "Then let's go win us a Battle of the Bands!" she said, trying to build some energy and enthusiasm.

But Twilight Sparkle's eye was twitching again.

Backstage Backbiting

★ ✴ ★

The gym was packed. The musical groups who were competing were clustered near the edge of the stage, nervously reviewing their sets and warming up. The air was crackling with anticipation and anxiety.

Principal Celestia and Vice Principal

Luna stepped onstage, microphones in hand. "Welcome to the first-ever Canterlot High School Battle of the Bands. I believe I speak for everyone when I say it is by far the greatest thing we have ever done here at this school." Principal Celestia spoke with a mechanical flatness, as if reading from a script.

Still there were hoots and hollers from the different bands. Flash Sentry raised his fist in the air.

"We are so glad our three newest students encouraged us to turn this event into something much more exciting than a boring old musical showcase," continued Principal Celestia. She gazed admiringly at Adagio Dazzle, Sonata Dusk, and Aria Blaze.

Vice Principal Luna coughed into her microphone to get everyone's attention. "But, as this is now a competition, we can only choose one winner." The expression on her face was almost cruel. "Who's it going to be?"

Almost at once, the room erupted with bickering.

"You don't stand a chance!"

"Your band stinks and you know it!"

"Don't talk the talk when you know you can't rock the rock."

Everyone was in one another's faces shouting and screaming. The audience was getting in on it, too, yelling out not only who they thought should win but who they wanted to lose.

"Losers! Losers! Losers!" one group of girls began chanting. They pointed at the

Rainbooms as they hurried into the gym at the last minute, their instruments in their hands.

Amid it all, unseen, the sickly green light oozed and wafted. It snaked its way toward Adagio, Sonata, and Aria. The pendants on their necks grew brighter and brighter.

"You feel that, girls?" said Adagio, reveling in the chaos. "Our true power is being restored!"

Aria and Sonata giggled uncontrollably.

"And that's before we've tapped into the strongest magic here," exalted Adagio Dazzle. "But the Rainblossoms, or whatever they're called, aren't under our spell. They are just as capable of falling apart as any one else. They just need a little push in the *wrong* direction." She looked where the various bands were waiting to play. "I have a feeling everyone here is going to be lining up to give them a shove."

Green light was practically oozing from the mouths of the ill-tempered band members.

Sonata squealed as her pendant grew brighter. "Ooh! Tickles!"

The Equestria Girls were carefully watching the Sirens from across the room.

"It's like they're...feeding off the negative energy," observed Rainbow Dash.

Twilight nodded her head. "That's *exactly* what they're doing. We have to get to the finals and perform the counterspell."

Fluttershy was wringing her hands. "I am so..."

"Nervicited?" guessed Pinkie Pie.

"Terrified!"

All the girls were. Fluttershy was just the one who was showing it the most.

Principal Celestia and Vice Principal Luna had taken seats at the judges' table in front of the stage. They visibly winced as Snips and Snails began performing a rap they had written.

"*They call me MC Snips, and that ain't no lie. My favorite food is pumpkin pie,*" exclaimed Snips.

"*I'm DJ Snazzy Snails. I like whales. When I go to the beach, I always bring my pails,*" added his partner.

"*Everybody knows my favorite color is orange. My rhymes are so fly, they're better than—*"

"*—an orange!*" finished Snails as the boys began beatboxing and making percussive noises with their mouths, although mostly they just sounded kind of strange and a little rude. As they finished, they dropped their mikes. It was just about the worst rap anyone in the room had ever heard, and a lot of people were saying so.

"Please do not drop the microphones!" announced Principal Celestia.

The boys grabbed them and left the stage, showing off to the Rainbooms as they passed. "In yo' face, Rainbooms!" said Snips, giving Snails a high five.

Applejack waited until they moved on and then whispered to the others, "Least we know one group who won't stand in the way of us getting to the finals."

Rainbow Dash strapped on her guitar. "Aw, yeah. Let's get ready to rock."

"Wait!" said Pinkie Pie in a sudden panic. "Where's Rarity?" She had just noticed that she was missing.

"I'm here! I'm here!" came a voice from across the gym. Rarity was running across the room toward her bandmates. She was dressed like a hippie with a long skirt and a metallic fringed blouse. It was Bohemian chic at its finest. Her friends' eyes widened as she approached. "We are in a competition in which we will be performing in front of an audience. I'm *not* going to wear something fabulous?"

None of the girls said a word. There wasn't time. They were expected onstage, and they had to get their instruments set up and tuned one last time.

"Remember," said Twilight to them quietly. "We have to be good enough to make it through, but not so good we let the Sirens see the magic within us. They could realize we plan to use it against them."

Rainbow Dash nodded. "Got it. Be cool enough to win, but not so cool we end up showing off the whole ears and tails and rainbows thing." She thought for a moment, her hands on the strings of her guitar. "So…about twenty percent less cool."

Twilight almost laughed, despite her nervousness.

Pinkie Pie took her place behind her drum kit. She made sure the other girls were watching and picked up her drumsticks. "One…two…one, two, three, four," she said, counting everyone in.

The girls launched into one of the school's favorite Sonic Rainboom songs.

Twilight was tapping her tambourine against her thigh and singing perfect backup harmony. Rainbow Dash belted out the lyrics. They were sounding really good. Maybe too good. Maybe too cool.

But the Rainbooms were so wrapped up

in their music that they didn't notice Photo Finish and her friends looking down at them from the rafters. On Photo Finish's command, her bandmates lowered a pair of magnets toward the stage. They were trying to interfere with the girls' playing by connecting with one of the instruments, but the magnets caught first on the metallic fringe of Rarity's blouse!

Rarity's arms lifted into the air, unable to play her keytar. It was like she was a marionette controlled by invisible strings. Applejack, distracted, missed a note.

Pinkie Pie was watching the audience while she played, but she was stunned to see Apple Bloom pretending to sleep through their performance. "Boring!" she yawned. How could their classmates—even their own relatives—be so unkind to fellow performers? Pinkie Pie's eyes narrowed. Drumming with only one hand now, she used the other to produce a small cannon! With a quick pull of a string, an explosion of rainbow-colored confetti rained down on the audience. But the confetti also landed on the Rainbooms!

A tiny piece of pastel confetti stuck to Twilight's tongue, and she spit it out. Just as she looked up, she saw Flash Sentry glaring at her. Why? Did he hate her? Did he think she was disgusting? What was the matter? He turned his back on her and stormed out of the gym. Twilight felt terrible.

Even worse, Snips and Snails were shining a harsh spotlight on Fluttershy. No matter where she moved onstage, it followed her. She felt embarrassed and self-conscious. It made her not want to perform at all. As she started singing off-key, Snips and Snails started to laugh.

Rarity yanked her arms down, and as she did, the fabric of her blouse ripped. "My metallic fringe!" she shrieked.

"Forget the fringe and just play!" hissed Applejack under her breath.

But the song was over, and the girls fumbled the last notes and bowed. As fast as they could, they hurried off the stage. Sunset and Spike were waiting for them.

"Ruined. Absolutely ruined!" wailed Rarity, still upset about her shirt.

Applejack was fuming. "Rarity! Were you tryin' to make us lose out there?"

"That was not my fault. This was an act of sabotage!"

"Yeah, well, whoever did this couldn't have done this if you didn't insist on dressing like…like this!" answered Applejack. "We need to *SOUND* good. Is there some reason that concept seems to escape you?"

Rainbow Dash was equally furious. "And what was with the confetti, Pinkie Pie? How am I supposed to shred if there's paper stuck in my frets?"

"It was pretty distracting," whined Fluttershy.

Pinkie Pie sniffed. "Says the girl who was running from a light the whole time. A light!"

Sunset Shimmer had never seen her friends being so unkind to one another. She tried to soothe their ruffled feelings. So much was at stake. No wonder they were stressed out. "You still sounded much better than most of the other bands. I'm sure you'll make it to the next round." But another thought had occurred to her. "It won't matter if you don't have that counter-spell ready, though."

"She's right," agreed Spike nervously.

Twilight's eye began twitching again.

Sunset Shimmer took control. "You all find a place to practice where the Sirens can't hear you. I'll keep an eye on things around here."

"I don't think we should use a class-room," said Twilight Sparkle.

She came around the corner and bumped right into Flash Sentry, who was leaning against a locker, strumming his guitar. Twilight laughed nervously. "We really, really need to stop bumping into each other like this."

Flash didn't look up. "You guys hear

something?" he said to the boys lounging around beside him. His bandmates shrugged, and he ignored Twilight. "Yeah. Me neither."

In a loud, clear voice, Twilight shouted, "I said, *WE HAVE TO STOP…*"

"There it is again," said Flash Sentry to the other boys. "So annoying." He went back to tuning his guitar and refused to look at Twilight.

She was astounded. This wasn't the boy she knew! "Why are you acting like this? I thought we were friends."

Flash Sentry's cold, dark eyes met hers. "And then you decided to come back here just so you could beat me in the Battle of the Bands. I want this, Twilight. And you're trying to take it from me. Some friend."

"That's not why…" Twilight Sparkle began to explain, but it was no use. Flash was ignoring her again.

"Come on, Twilight," said Applejack gently. "We've got things to do." She pulled her away down the hallway.

Flash called out as the girls disappeared. "You really think you're going to help them? I bet you have no idea what you're even doing."

His words struck Twilight deep in her heart. Not only did Flash hate her, he'd said out loud what most frightened her. Tears welled up in her eyes, but she quickly tried to wipe them away.

The Sirens were coming around the corner. One look at Twilight Sparkle's face, and they knew that they were already winning.

"Tears already? This is only the first round," Adagio Dazzle said smugly.

Over the loudspeaker, Principal Celestia announced the next band.

"Better head back," said Adagio to her companions. "We're supposed to go on next."

They began to saunter down the hallway, but their way was blocked by Sunset Shimmer. Her hands were on her hips, and she was ready to stare down the Sirens. "You're never going to get away with this," she warned them.

"Why?" said Adagio smoothly. "Because you didn't? Oh. We know all about you, Sunset. You've got quite the reputation at Canterlot High."

Sunset stood her ground. "I've changed. I'm in a much better place now."

Aria Blaze laughed contemptuously. "Waiting in the wings while your 'friends' have all the fun onstage?"

"Oh yes," snickered Adagio. "You girls are *so* tight. And yet, they didn't even ask you to be in the band."

Aria raised a single arched eyebrow. "Probably afraid no one would want to see them play if she was in the group."

"Too bad. So sad," said Sonata with fake sympathy.

Sunset Shimmer was beginning to lose her bravado. All the things they were saying were actually kind of true.

"If it's any consolation"—Adagio laughed—"no one is going to remember you at all, by the time we're done." She brushed past Sunset with a smug smile, and the other two girls followed her back to the gym.

Sunset watched them go, but she couldn't move. She felt broken and alone. She wasn't in the Sonic Rainbooms, she couldn't even help them, and no one would ever forget how bad she'd been. She felt worse now than she had even after the terrible disaster last fall. Then she had just lost a dream of power, but now she felt like she had just lost her first real friends.

Friendship unplugged

★ ★ ★

The Dazzlings were onstage and getting ready to perform. Adagio reminded the other Sirens not to go full blast until the final round. Offstage, bands had been sabotaging one another—hiding one another's instruments, breaking guitar strings, unplugging amps. The negative energy in the room had given the Sirens more power than ever, and they were using it to their advantage. They were entrancing. Their infectious music silenced the crowd and mesmerized them.

Oh, wha-oh, oh, wha-oh,
You didn't know that you fell.
Oh, wha-oh, oh, wha-oh,
Now that you're under our spell.

Blindsided by the beat,
clapping your hands,
stomping your feet.
You didn't know that you fell.
Oh, oh, oh, oh, oh, oh.

Now you've fallen under our spell.
Oh, oh, oh, oh, oh, oh.

We've got the music makes you move it,
Got the song that makes you lose it.
We say, "Jump," you say, "How high?"
Put your hands up to the sky.

Oh, wha-oh, oh, wha-oh,
You didn't know that you fell.
Oh, wha-oh, oh, wha-oh,
Now that you're under our spell.

Listen to the sound of my voice, ah, oh, ah, oh.
Soon you'll find you don't have a choice, ah,
    oh.
Captured in the web of my song, ah, oh, ah,
    oh.
Soon you'll all be singing along, oh.

Oh, wha-oh, oh, wha-oh,
You didn't know that you fell.

Oh, wha-oh, oh, wha-oh,
Now that you're under our spell.

Oh, wha-oh, oh, wha-oh,
You didn't know that you fell.
Oh, wha-oh, oh, wha-oh,
Now that you're under our spell.

None of the other groups were anywhere near as good as they were. Not Flash Sentry and his band. Not Apple Bloom and hers. No one. Not even the Rainbooms.

Crammed into a janitor's closet with her friends, Twilight Sparkle tried not to listen to the Sirens as she worked on her spell. Rainbow light flashed here and there and then sputtered out. One of the girls would briefly pony up, but then her tail or her pony ears would disappear. It just wasn't working.

Enthusiastic applause exploded in the gym, and the girls knew that the Dazzlings had finished their opening act. Back in the gym, Principal Celestia posted the names of the bands who had made it to the next round. Flash Sentry fumed when his name wasn't there. Other bands started complaining. The anger and distress made the Sirens' pendants glow. They had somehow already secured a place in the main event, but the Great and Powerful Trixie would be up against the Rainbooms for the other position.

Sunset Shimmer, who had been in the gym, shared all this with the girls. "This is it. Last round, and you're in the finals.

Unless you think the counterspell is ready to be played now?"

Twilight shook her head emphatically. No. No. No.

"Don't worry, Twilight," said Applejack. "Finals aren't until later. We'll get in a little more practice before we're supposed to hit the stage. We've just got to defeat Trixie and the Illusions to get there, and how hard can that be? We won't let you down."

Under her breath, Twilight repeated the words to herself. " 'You won't let me down.' " That wasn't what she was worried about. She was pretty sure she was going to be the one disappointing her friends.

Rarity dusted herself off and tried to be upbeat. "I'm sure getting a chance to practice without being surrounded by filthy mops and cleaning supplies will help."

As the girls left the janitor's closet, Fluttershy timidly approached Rainbow Dash. "Um, I was just wondering. We haven't played any of my songs yet...."

Rainbow Dash waved her away. "It's the semifinals. We gotta do 'Awesome as I Wanna Be'!"

"Don't know why I even asked," said Fluttershy with a frustrated sigh. She picked up her tambourine and headed to the gym with the other girls.

CHAPTER

16

Star Power

★ ★ ★

The Great and Powerful Trixie was strutting across the stage, her arms in the air, the microphone held up close to her mouth. She was impressive, and Principal Celestia and Vice Principal Luna were clapping enthusiastically from their seats. Even some of the bands who hadn't made it to the finals were cheering.

Trixie and the Illusions took an extra bow and then sauntered triumphantly off-stage past the Rainbooms.

"You're never going to top that performance, Rainbooms!" bragged Trixie. "Though if you ask me, you shouldn't even be allowed to try when you potentially have such a big advantage over the rest of us."

A proud smile spread across Rainbow Dash's face. "My superior guitar playing and off-the-charts awesome singing voice?"

"Don't be ridiculous," scoffed Trixie. "I mean *her.*" She pointed at Twilight Sparkle. "If you were really all that, Rainbow Dash, you wouldn't have needed to bring in some magical ringer to have half a chance." She smirked as she leaned closer and hissed, "*Everyone* is talking about it."

Rainbow Dash was used to playing it cool on the soccer field, and she didn't let Trixie see for one moment how much her words had upset her. "Please. I could win this thing as a solo act, and *everybody* knows it."

"Sure you could." Trixie laughed. She waved her hand, and a smokelike fog wrapped around her.

The Rainbooms were coughing and fanning away the smoke. When it had cleared, Trixie had disappeared.

"She's gone," said Pinkie Pie, impressed.

What could she be up to? But there was no time to figure that out. Principal Celestia was announcing the Rainbooms' next song. It was time for the girls to take the stage.

"Knock 'em dead, Rainbooms!" encouraged Spike.

"I'll be here. Just…watching," Sunset Shimmer whispered to herself.

Fluttershy looked almost as unhappy as Sunset. As they were getting ready onstage, she approached Rainbow Dash one more time about playing her song, but the guitarist ignored her. On the edge of tears, Fluttershy went back to her microphone.

Rainbow Dash hit the first notes of "Awesome as I Wanna Be," and each of the girls came in with her part perfectly. But then suddenly, Rainbow simply stopped singing and playing. She was staring out into the audience where Trixic was holding up a hand-drawn poster that showed a picture of a tiny Rainbow Dash overshadowed by an enormous singing Twilight Sparkle.

Furious, Rainbow Dash launched into an impromptu guitar solo, angrily strumming her guitar. She was wild, and she was also magnificent, playing like she'd never played before, sliding and bending notes, astonishing the crowd with her electrifying fretwork. She was so absorbed in her playing, so determined to be the best, to be better than Twilight, that she forgot they weren't supposed to let the Sirens see their real magic.

Her ears appeared. Her tail appeared. Her mane was lush and flowing. She was ponying up, and everyone was witnessing her transformation. Everyone. Adagio Dazzle's eyes narrowed as she realized just how powerful the girls' magic really was.

Panicked, Sunset rushed from the wings and crashed into Rainbow Dash, knocking her offstage. A dazed Rainbow Dash returned to normal. But it was too late. Adagio was already plotting her next move.

Even worse, the audience had misunderstood what Sunset had done. They were certain she was ruining the Rainbooms' performance. Trixie was clapping gleefully.

"Aw, yeah! That's the bad girl we love to hate!" yelled Flash Sentry.

"I knew she was still trouble!" shouted a girl.

"The real Sunset Shimmer is back!" The words were repeated throughout the room as if everyone had been just waiting for her evil self to appear. But that's not what had happened!

"No, no, no!" Sunset protested. "It isn't like that!" But how could she explain?

Even Spike was disappointed in her. "Great job."

Rainbow Dash turned on her. "What was that all about?"

"You were showing them your magic. I...I didn't know what else to do."

Rarity was furious. "Close the curtains! Unplug the amp! Give *us* a chance to deal with the situation!"

"I'm sorry. I just wanted to help." Sunset was on the edge of tears.

"Yeah, well, you didn't," said Rainbow Dash.

But true and steady Applejack wasn't fooled. She knew Rainbow Dash had really caused the trouble. "None of this would've happened if you weren't tryin' to show off. As usual."

Trixie sauntered backstage, delighted to see the girls bickering. "Good show, Rainbooms. I especially liked the part where Sunset Shimmer, in a fit of jealous rage, knocked out Rainbow Dash mid–guitar solo."

"It wasn't a fit of jealous rage!" exploded Sunset, her face red, her hands balled into fists. She almost looked like the she-demon she'd turned into last fall.

The Rainbooms were speechless.

Trixie just laughed. "If you say so." She was gloating as she turned to watch Principal Celestia taking center stage to announce which band was moving on to the finals with the Dazzlings. Trixie pulled out a compact and checked her makeup. She was ready to run up as soon as Principal Celestia called her name. "I'm guessing it wasn't too difficult a decision!"

But just as Principal Celestia was about to make her announcement, the Sirens leaned in close to her and Vice Principal Luna and began softly singing in their ears. The words were too quiet for anyone to make out, but their effect was immediately clear. The women's faces went blank briefly before they began speaking in unison. "We've never wanted anything more!" they said in a kind of trance.

Sunset was watching them and trying to figure out what was going on, but the Rainbooms, who were convinced they weren't going to the finals, were too upset to even listen.

"What can we do?" wailed Rarity. "There

isn't going to be another opportunity for us to play. And I had the most gorgeous outfit for the finals."

"Yep," said Applejack sarcastically, "'cause that's the real tragedy here, that you won't get to play dress-up."

"You know perfectly well that is not what I meant!"

"You guys want to keep it down?" hushed Rainbow Dash. She had just enough faith in her own playing, even with Sunset's interruption, to think there was a chance they'd made it.

"Who are you kidding? You know it isn't going to be us." Tears welled up in Flutter-shy's eyes.

"The band that will be joining the Dazzlings in tonight's finals is..." Even before Principal Celestia had finished speaking,

Trixie, waving to the crowd, was taking the stage. As if on cue, Principal Celestia and Vice Principal Luna announced the name of the winning band, "…the Sonic Rainbooms!"

"What?!" screeched Trixie.

Pinkie Pie was jumping up and down and squealing. "Did they just say the Rainbooms?"

Trixie pushed past her in a huff, her face twisted into a mask of fury. "This isn't over," she warned.

Confused and surprised, the Rainbooms walked out onstage. Sure, they hadn't played badly in the beginning, but then Rainbow Dash had jammed on her own and the whole song had been ruined by Sunset Shimmer. As if to confirm these feelings, their appearance onstage was met by boos from the crowd. It was strange and embarrassing.

"Congratulations, girls. You deserve it," said Principal Celestia.

"Seriously?!" questioned Pinkie Pie. "We didn't even finish our—"

Rainbow Dash elbowed Pinkie Pie in the ribs. They'd made it. That's all that mattered.

"See you at the big show, Rainbooms," called out Adagio Dazzle. "We are *really* looking forward to it."

"Not as much as we are!" said Rainbow Dash. There was going to be no holding back. She was ready to rock and ready to win!

Dis-Chords

★ ★ ★

The Battle of the Bands had left crowds of kids feeling defeated and unhappy. They didn't want to celebrate the Sonic Rainbooms' success. They were jealous.

"Never should have been you, Rainbooms!" Photo Finish shouted at them as they made their way through the gym.

"I am a classically trained musician. It should have been me!" pouted Octavia.

Sweetie Belle glared at Rarity. "Thanks a lot, Rarity! Now my friends and I will never be the rock stars we were obviously meant to be! All because of you."

There were angry stares and muttered insults. Bad feelings filled the room.

"Worst. Sister. Ever," hissed Apple Bloom to Applejack.

But the most upset of all was Trixie. She was throwing a total temper tantrum. "This is a travesty. A travesty!"

Adagio Dazzle sidled up beside her and expressed sympathy. "It really is! The Rainbooms don't deserve to be in the finals. Not when your band was so much better in the semis."

"And wanted it so much more," Aria Blaze added, fueling Trixie's anger.

"Alas, this is the way it's going to be. The Dazzlings versus the Rainbooms," said Adagio. She was reveling in all the hostility and misery that she'd created.

"Unless, of course," said Sonata Dusk, barely realizing what she was saying, "the Rainbooms don't manage to make it to their set. They could be held up for some reason, couldn't they?"

A wicked smile lit up Trixie's face. It was time to get working!

CHAPTER

18

Off the Charts (and under the Stage)

★ ★ ★

The final showdown between the two bands was going to take place at Canterlot High's outdoor amphitheater. The Rainbooms had a lot to get ready, and Sunset Shimmer was lending a hand, eager to let her friends know that she hadn't meant to disrupt their performance—only save their magic secrets.

Spike was busy, too—adjusting amps, tuning instruments, and helping Pinkie Pie find her lost drumsticks. Which she'd used to put up her hair. Everyone was so busy. But Fluttershy was trying to figure out what had really happened. "This doesn't make any sense. We were awful. Doesn't anybody else think it's strange that we're the ones who made it to the finals?"

A voice from beside the stage agreed with her. "Very strange."

"What are you doing here, Trixie?" asked Rainbow Dash. "Pretty sure the losers are supposed to be up there in the cheap seats."

"The Great and Powerful Trixie is the most talented girl at Canterlot High. It is I who deserves to be in the finals. And I will not be denied!" With a flourish, she pulled a hidden lever—and the stage floor beneath the Rainbooms opened!

Spike managed to leap onto a backstage speaker, but Sunset Shimmer, Twilight, Pinkie Pie, Rainbow Dash, Rarity, Fluttershy, Applejack, and all their instruments fell into the hole beneath the stage.

"Aaaahhh!" they shouted.

"See you never!" yelled Trixie. She pulled another lever, and the trapdoor closed. The girls were locked beneath the stage.

"Told you someone would give them a shove," said Adagio Dazzle, who had been watching from the back of the amphitheater.

Sonata Dusk looked confused. "She didn't shove them. She pulled a lever."

"Go back to sleep, Sonata," sneered Aria Blaze.

Underneath the stage, it was almost

completely dark. A small shaft of light came through a gap that let the girls glimpse the seats in the theater, which were quickly filling with kids who had come to watch the show. But there didn't seem to be any way out. The girls were frantic. All the doors were locked tight! Rainbow Dash hurled herself against them but slammed to the ground with a thud. There was no way out.

Above them, the girls could hear shuffling feet, the high-pitched whirs of feedback from amps being readied, and the tuning of guitars. Then they heard actual music and singing. It was Trixie and the Illusions. She was taking their place with her band!

Of all the girls, the most defeated was Twilight. "Maybe it doesn't even matter that we're trapped down here. I don't think the counterspell was even going to work."

"Course it would've worked, Twilight," said Applejack. "Assumin' a certain band member didn't try to hog the spotlight the whole time we were tryin' to play it."

"Hey!" Rainbow Dash snapped. "If you want to tell Twilight she's getting a little too caught up in trying to be the new leader of this band, you don't have to be all cryptic about it."

Rarity corrected her. "She was talking about you, Rainbow Dash."

Rainbow Dash couldn't believe it. "*Me?* I'm just trying to make sure my band rocks as hard as we need to rock."

"*Our* band!" all the girls corrected her.

Onstage, Trixie was hitting the high notes of her finale.

"Try to top that!" she shouted to Adagio Dazzle after she'd taken her bows.

Adagio pretended to be worried. "Oh, gosh, I don't know if we can."

Sonata and Aria giggled as they followed Adagio onto the stage. The girls picked up their guitars, tested their microphones, and gazed out at the audience. No, they weren't just an audience, they were fans...and they were about to become their blindly obedient subjects.

"We're the Dazzlings," said Adagio, her voice deep and husky. "Prepare to be mesmerized."

Aria's slow, heavy bass line created a hypnotic rhythm. Sonata offered up a haunting harmony while Adagio began to work her seductive magic. All eyes were on them. Everyone was listening to them. Their music was entrancing.

But not to the girls stuck beneath the

stage. Twilight was not lost in reverie. She was panicking! Her hair was a frazzled mess, both eyes were twitching now, and she was pacing back and forth on all fours as if she'd forgotten she was a human and thought she was a pony again.

"But why isn't it working?" she fretted. "I should know what to do. How can I not know what to do? How can I have failed like this?"

The girls were upset and fighting with one another. Applejack was furious at Rainbow Dash for hijacking the band. "It might've been your idea to start a band, but it's not just your band, Rainbow Dash." She stamped her foot.

"I'm the one who writes all the songs!" yelled Rainbow Dash.

"I write songs!" said a frustrated Fluttershy. "You just never let us play any of them."

"I had the most perfect ensembles for us to wear," Rarity moaned.

"Again with the costumes?!" fumed Applejack. "No one cares what we're wearing!"

Rarity's eyes flashed. "I care, Applejack. So sorry if I enjoy trying to make a creative contribution to the band."

Pinkie Pie was distraught. "Hey, anybody here remember fun? I'll give you a hint. It's the exact opposite of being in the Sonic Rainbooms lately."

"I wish I'd never asked any of you to be in this band." Rainbow Dash was seething with anger.

"I wish I'd never agreed to be in it!" cried Rarity.

"Me neither!" added Fluttershy and Applejack.

The girls were all so upset they didn't

notice the green light that had begun to flicker and glow as they fought. As their voices grew louder, the light grew brighter. Sickening puces, ugly khakis, vile olives—they were the colors of jealousy and envy and distrust, and they formed a hideous rainbow over the heads of the Equestria Girls. Sunset Shimmer noticed it with alarm, but no one would listen to her. They were all too busy arguing.

The swirling rainbow wafted up through the cracks in the stage floor where the Dazzlings were playing. Their pendants absorbed the hateful energy. They pulsed and glowed. The Dazzlings sang with more power than ever. The audience was rapt.

Sunset knew she had to do something. She stepped in between her friends and shouted at the top of her voice, "Stop! You have to stop!"

Even louder than her voice, though, was the hypnotic sound of the Dazzlings. Their song penetrated every nook and cranny of the amphitheater. Everything was falling under their spell.

"This is what they've been after all along," Sunset said. "They've wanted to provoke you. They've needed you to fight. That's how they're feeding off the magic inside you!"

The Dazzlings' music was becoming more and more enrapturing. Their pendants were growing brighter and brighter. All of a sudden, a shimmering explosion of scarlet light came from each of them. The Sirens were transformed! They were no longer just girls, but girls with the magical Equestrian spirit. Their ears, their wings, their tails—they were beautiful and they were terrible. Everyone who saw them was ready to worship them and do whatever they asked.

"We love you, Dazzlings!"

"You're amazing!"

"I live to serve you, Dazzlings!"

"Dazzlings! Dazzlings! Dazzlings!"

Another burst of red light from the Sirens' pendants sent a sonic wave exploding over the amphitheater and spread the Sirens' magic like an evil fog across the entire town!

A Rainbow Reunion

***

"We adore you!"

"We love you!"

"We worship you! We'll do anything for you!"

The voices of adulation were coming not just from the crowd, but all around town. The Dazzlings were creating an army of obedient slaves—and they were doing it using the Equestria Girls' own Magic of Friendship.

The Rainbooms were horrified.

"How can they be using our magic?" Applejack wondered. "It's the Magic of Friendship, and they don't understand anything about friendship."

But Sunset Shimmer had been thinking about everything very carefully. "Ever since you started this band, you've been letting little things get to you. I never said anything because I didn't feel like it was my place. Not when I was so new to this whole friendship thing." She took a breath. She didn't want to seem arrogant or all-knowing. "I still have a lot to learn, but I do know that if you don't work out even the smallest problems right at the start, the Magic of Friendship can be turned into . . . well, something else."

No one said anything for a moment. They were too embarrassed. Here was Sunset, who supposedly didn't know anything about friendship, explaining to them how to get along with one another.

Twilight Sparkle was particularly disappointed in herself. She was the Princess of Friendship, after all. "I can't believe all this tension was happening right under my nose, and I didn't realize it. I'm supposed to be the one with all the answers, and all I've done since I got here is let you down." She hung her head in shame.

But Sunset had come to understand many things over the past few days. She knew exactly what it was like to think you were the best, the one and only, the top of the top. It was a very lonely place. "I don't think anyone is supposed to have all the answers. But you *can* count on your friends to help you find them."

Her wise words filled Twilight Sparkle with joy. "I think you already have found the answer," she said to Sunset Shimmer. "Come on! We need to get out of here."

One more time, the girls rushed to the door, desperately pulling at it. But it was no use. It was still locked. How were they going to get out?

That was the exact moment when the door miraculously opened. Standing there were Spike and DJ Pon-3, holding a crowbar in her hands. She'd pried the door open!

Twilight hugged Spike.

"Sorry I took so long," he apologized. "I had to find somebody who wasn't under the Sirens' spell to help me get you out."

DJ Pon-3 waved at all the girls.

"Why *isn't* she under their spell?" wondered Twilight out loud.

"Never takes off her headphones!" said Spike, pointing at them.

DJ Pon-3 smiled and gave the girls a thumbs-up sign. They all laughed out loud with relief. But not for long. They had work to do. Grabbing their instruments, they ran out of the cellar toward the parking lot, where DJ Pon-3's car was waiting.

As DJ Pon-3 raced toward a nearby hillside, the girls were frightened as the sky turned darker and darker red. The Sirens' evil spell was spreading! Even from the car, they could hear the hypnotic music.

The girls got out of the car when they reached the landmark overlooking the whole town. They were ready to play the counter-spell. But there was only one problem. They had nowhere to plug in their instruments.

"How are we supposed to play over them from up here?" Rainbow Dash cried.

DJ Pon-3 noticed the girls looking around and figured out what the problem was immediately. Good thing she had a pair of enormous speakers in the trunk of her car! She never went anywhere without them.

"Sweet!" Rainbow Dash exclaimed when she saw them.

"Come on, y'all, time to prove we've still got the Magic of Friendship inside us," said Applejack.

Twilight Sparkle stepped forward. At last, she knew the counterspell. "And there's only one way to do it."

"We're getting the band back together?!"
squealed Pinkie Pie.

"We're getting *our* band back together,"
said Rainbow Dash.

The girls shared a sweet smile. They were
a team again.

"Just one question," asked Rarity. "Which
version of the counterspell are we going to
play? You had us rehearse quite a few ver-
sions as I recall."

"All this time, I thought I had to be the
one to come up with a musical counterspell.
I thought I had to do everything. But I don't
think it matters what song we play. As long
as we play it together. As friends."

An idea lit up Rainbow Dash's face. "In
that case, I know just the song."

Applejack was just starting to roll her

eyes when she realized what Rainbow Dash was suggesting.

"Fluttershy's written a really great song," said Rainbow Dash.

Fluttershy beamed with happiness.

"I know just the song you're talking about," said Twilight. She'd seen it in the notebook Fluttershy had loaned her.

"Just one last thing," said Applejack. "We're about to save the world here. Personally, I think we should do it in style. Rarity, I don't suppose...?"

Rarity was delighted. "I thought you'd never ask."

Battle of the Bands

★ ★ ★

The Dazzlings heard it before anyone else—
music with a magic more powerful than
theirs. It was easier to listen to and more fun.
It made you want to find a friend and dance,
not gaze into space like a zombie. Already
people in the audience were responding to

it. They were smiling more naturally and saying nice things to one another.

Adagio Dazzle looked all around the amphitheater, but she couldn't see the Rainbooms anywhere. That's when Aria Blaze pointed to the distant hillside.

"So the Rainbooms want to turn this into a real Battle of the Bands?" Adagio was steely-eyed with determination. "Okay, then. Let's battle!"

The Dazzlings' pendants glowed brighter for an instant, and the girls used their wings to take to the sky. They swooped over the crowd and headed right toward the Rainbooms. Beneath them kids were pointing and shouting, but the Dazzlings weren't listening. They were going to defeat their enemies.

The Rainbooms were ready for them!

They had one another, and they had the Magic of Friendship. They were in full pony mode and ready to use their cutie marks in their defense.

Every time Pinkie Pie hit her snare drum, her bass drum would fire balloons just like a cannon. When Fluttershy slapped her tambourine against her leg, butterflies miraculously emerged and swarmed around the Dazzlings, confusing them. Every thump of Applejack's bass let loose a barrage of apples. Rarity's keytar exploded with diamonds whose sparkling surfaces momentarily blinded the Dazzlings. Rainbow Dash's guitar shot rainbow-shaped bolts that sent the Dazzlings diving. Balloons, butterflies, apples, diamonds, and rainbows—in the right hands and with plenty of teamwork, they were a powerful defense.

Still, despite being conked in the head and spun around and confused, the Dazzlings kept on fighting. Their scarlet pendants created a laser light show with flashing beams of color that hurt the Rainbooms' eyes. They couldn't keep playing in the glare. It was making them dizzy and disoriented.

Twilight Sparkle was desperate. "Sunset Shimmer! We need you!" she called.

Sunset stepped close to her friend and began singing the chorus to Fluttershy's song. Her voice was clear as a bell and beautiful. She knew every word. She hit every note. The more she sang, the greater the magic became. She felt her ears arrive first. Next, her tail began swinging back and forth, and then she sprouted wings! She could pony up, too!

Even better, she had her own special powers just like the Rainbooms. From her voice came swirling suns that encircled the Dazzlings and trapped them!

Sunset Shimmer sang and sang. But she was no longer singing alone. Voices from the amphitheater and all around town joined her song. Fluttershy was singing. Twilight Sparkle and Rainbow Dash were singing. Everyone was singing. Everyone was experiencing the wonder of harmony.

As the song reached its crescendo, an ethereal Alicorn appeared in the sky like a royal constellation. Her graceful unicorn horn pointed to the stars. Her magical wings wafted an unearthly perfume across the land. All of a sudden, white light shot out of her unicorn horn toward the Dazzlings.

It blew them right across town, right back to the stage. They were nothing more than ordinary teenage girls again.

The crowd went wild as the Rainbooms and Sunset Shimmer lifted into the air. As they gently landed on the stage beside the Sirens, they played the final notes of Fluttershy's oh-so-special song.

Curtain Calls

✷ ✷ ✷

The Sirens were cowering. Their arms were over their heads. They didn't know what was going to happen next, but they were pretty sure it was going to be bad. After all, if they had defeated the Rainbooms, they would have been just awful to them.

But Sunset Shimmer mostly felt pity for them. She reached down and, one by one, removed the red-jewel pendants from around their necks. The Sirens scrambled to their feet, still trying to regain the adoration of the crowd.

They began singing, *"You will adore us. This much we know is true. You will adore us. Before this song is through."*

Every note was off, and the Sirens were so completely tone-deaf that the crowd began to boo them off the stage.

Sunset Shimmer looked at the pendants in her hand. "Guess that explains why these were so special to them."

"Without those pendants and the magic you brought here from Equestria, they're just three harmless teenage girls," said Twilight Sparkle.

Just then, Twilight Sparkle was reminded that she was also a teenage girl—at least for the moment.

Flash Sentry, freed from the Sirens' enchantment, was running over to the stage. "That was amazing! Rainbooms rule!" he said. He bounded up beside the girls and wrapped Twilight in an embrace. She blushed three different shades of pink.

Trixie was glaring at her. "You may have vanquished the Dazzlings, but you will never have the amazing, showstopping ability of the Great and Powerful Trixie." She waved her arms and conjured a poof of smoke. When it cleared, the girls could see her running out of the amphitheater. Rainbow Dash wanted to fly after her and tell her to behave herself, but Twilight stopped her.

"Someday she'll learn," said Twilight in her most princesslike voice. "She just needs to be given a chance."

Her eyes met Sunset Shimmer's. People

made mistakes, but they could also change for the better. And friends understood that. Sunset found herself in the center of a group hug with all her best friends—Twilight, Applejack, Rarity, Fluttershy, Rainbow Dash, and Pinkie Pie.

"You know, Twilight is going back to Equestria soon," said Rainbow Dash. "The Rainbooms could really use someone to help Fluttershy on backup vocals."

Sunset Shimmer was glowing. "I also play the guitar!"

"We'll see," teased Rainbow Dash, grinning. But Rainbow Dash had learned a lesson, too. If she was really going to lead the band, she was going to have to recognize and celebrate everyone's special talents.

CHAPTER

22

Rave Reviews for the Rainbooms!

★ ✶ ★

The next day was filled with music and celebration. Finally, the girls got to sit down with Twilight Sparkle and share a few months' worth of gossip. Rainbow Dash told her about soccer and basketball games. Rarity gave her a fashion show. Fluttershy introduced her to her newest pets. And Pinkie? Pinkie Pie just laughed with happiness to have all her friends together.

But it couldn't stay like that. Twilight Sparkle had a kingdom back in Equestria, and the ponies there needed her. Besides, now that she had reopened the portal, she could visit from time to time. This wasn't good-bye forever. But it was still hard.

In the afternoon, all the friends gathered around the Wondercolt statue.

"Sure wish you could stay longer," sighed Applejack.

"Me too," said Twilight Sparkle, "but I have responsibilities in Equestria that I have to get back to. Its citizens need me. But this isn't good-bye. It's good-bye until next time."

All the girls hugged her. Sunset gave her

a special embrace. There were tears in her eyes. She had learned so much from Twilight Sparkle, and her life was so different now.

Twilight picked up Spike. "Ready?"

"Ready."

The two of them stepped into the portal.

White light flashed while streaks of vibrant color stretched and squashed and bent Twilight Sparkle and Spike back into a pony and a dragon. With a final burst of light, they arrived in Twilight's library in Equestria.

Applejack, Fluttershy, Rainbow Dash, Pinkie Pie, and Rarity—Twilight Sparkle's favorite ponies—were waiting for them.

"Tell us everything!" said Rainbow Dash, trotting over.

"Whatja see?" asked Applejack.

"What did you do?" asked Fluttershy.

"What did you wear?" said Rarity.

But Pinkie Pie, as always, asked the most important question of all. "What did you learn?"

Twilight took a deep breath, thinking of all the events from the past few days. "I learned that I still have a lot to learn. I'm the Princess of Friendship now, and lots of ponies are going to be looking to me to solve their problems. But it was foolish of me to think that I should have all the answers." She looked into the eyes of each of the ponies and smiled. "What I do have are good friends who will always be there to help me find them."

Rarity whinnied. "Well then, I think we should get started right away. You've had quite a bit of mail since you've been gone."

She pointed at an enormous mountain of bags filled with letters.

Seeing them, Pinkie Pie took a flying leap right into the middle of the pile. She emerged a moment later, flipping through envelopes. "From Las Pegasus, Baltimare, Fillydelphia…"

There were so many letters and so many responsibilities. But Twilight Sparkle was ready, thanks to her friends at Canterlot High and thanks to Sunset Shimmer. Once they had been enemies and now they would be best friends forever, wherever they were.

Far away in another world, Sunset was thinking about Twilight. She was writing to her in the magic journal while she waited in the music room for the girls to arrive.

Dear Princess Twilight, Sunset Shimmer wrote. *Missing you already and hope you'll be back soon. Things are definitely looking up for me here at Canterlot High, but I know I still have a lot to learn about friendship. Hope you don't mind if I write to you for advice when I need it. Your friend, Sunset Shimmer*

Sunset closed the journal and put it in her backpack as Rainbow Dash and the other girls bounded into the music room. "You ready or what?"

"I'm ready!" Sunset laughed, grabbing her guitar.

Fluttershy picked up her tambourine, and Rarity strapped on her keytar. Rainbow Dash and Applejack got ready to jam, and Pinkie Pie settled in behind her drum kit.

"One…two…one, two, three, four!" called out Pinkie Pie, cueing all the girls.

The Sonic Rainbooms were ready to rock!

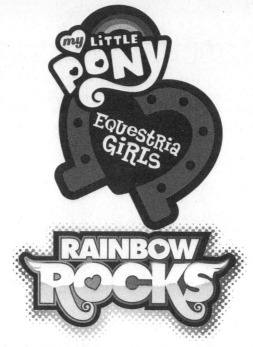

The Sonic Rainbooms' music is magic, and
every time they perform, their rainbow energy
shines through Canterlot High! Even when
disharmony prevails, the ponies prove they
still have the Magic of Friendship within.
Turn the page to share your experiences
of friendship and magic.

BaLancinG tHe BanD

Being in a band is just like friendship.
It requires teamwork and harmony to thrive.
Sometimes, though, your friendships may
experience discord. What causes friction
among your friends? Write about it here.

_____

_____

_____

_____

_____

_____

_____

_____

_____

Elements of Harmony

Why do you think you and your friends jam so well together? Write about your Elements of Harmony and how they will help your band succeed.

_____

_____

_____

_____

_____

_____

_____

_____

Fund-Raising With Friends

Principal Celestia beams at her students' enthusiasm for participating in the musical showcase and suggests they use this opportunity to raise money for after-school programs! List some ideas for raising money for after-school programs at your own school.

_____

_____

_____

_____

_____

_____

MUSICAL MOODS

Have you ever noticed how a song's tempo
and lyrics affect your mood? Some songs
lift you up, while others bring you down.
List some songs and describe how they
make you feel when listening to them.

_____

_____

_____

_____

_____

_____

_____

_____

Lyrical Laughter

Below is a set of lyrics sung by the Dazzlings at the Canterlot High School Musical Showcase! Use you lyrical talents to write the next verse!

"Now you've fallen under our spell.

Oh, oh, oh, oh, oh, oh.

We've got the music makes you move it,

Got the song that makes you lose it.

We say, 'Jump,' you say, 'How high?'

Put your hands up to the sky.

Oh, wha-oh, oh, wha-oh,

You didn't know that you fell.

Oh, wha-oh, oh, wha-oh,

Now that you're under our spell."

PResto PosteR!

Create two compelling posters to get Canterlot High excited for the mane event: the Battle of the Bands! One poster for the Dazzlings and one for the Sonic Rainbooms!

A Jumbled Ensemble

Can you help the Sonic Rainbooms
and the Dazzlings by finding their names
in this Battle of the Bands word search?

```
E  L  K  R  A  P  S  T  H  G  I  L  I  W  T
F  Y  T  I  R  A  R  W  K  K  X  R  M  S  Y
W  O  F  P  A  P  P  L  E  J  A  C  K  I  C
Q  F  S  O  N  A  T  A  D  U  S  K  Z  W  X
B  A  T  T  L  E  E  I  P  E  I  K  N  I  P
L  H  G  I  H  T  O  L  R  E  T  N  A  C  O
H  O  Y  K  Q  N  A  R  I  A  B  L  A  Z  E
B  I  H  H  T  W  B  X  B  Q  O  E  V  V  H
T  G  E  W  V  N  L  J  H  U  E  G  A  R  S
O  A  P  B  M  G  H  U  B  U  S  N  I  X  H
O  D  G  S  G  N  I  L  Z  Z  A  D  Z  E  A
F  A  B  U  M  K  E  D  J  M  Q  R  Y  E  W
X  R  A  I  N  B  O  W  D  A  S  H  F  O  N
A  S  O  N  I  C  R  A  I  N  B  O  O  M  S
I  W  Y  H  S  R  E  T  T  U  L  F  K  A  P
```

ADAGIO

APPLEJACK

ARIA BLAZE

BATTLE

CANTERLOT HIGH

DAZZLINGS

FLUTTERSHY

PINKIE PIE

RAINBOW DASH

RARITY

SONATA DUSK

SONIC RAINBOOMS

TWILIGHT SPARKLE

In Need of a Tune-Up

Do you know a group of friends like the Dazzlings—peers who are competitive for the wrong reasons? Friends who throw temper tantrums when they don't win or get their way? Write about them here.

_____

_____

_____

_____

_____

_____

_____

_____

Have you ever acted like Rainbow Dash or the Dazzlings? List some ideas of how you can be competitive in a positive way!

_____

_____

_____

_____

_____

_____

_____

_____

_____

_____

_____

SHOWSTOPPING STYLE

The Dazzlings and the Sonic Rainbooms want
to stand out from each other onstage.